SHANNON: CARRYING THE STAR

SHANNON: CARRYING THE STAR

•

Charles E. Friend

AVALON BOOKS
NEW YORK

PRINTED IN THE UNITED STATES OF AMERICA
ON ACID-FREE PAPER
BY HADDON CRAFTSMEN, BLOOMSBURG, PENNSYLVANIA

This story is dedicated to the famous Kansas trail towns of the 19th century—places like Abilene, Caldwell, Dodge City, Ellsworth, Wichita—and to the great western lawmen who "carried the star" in those towns. Together they wrote an unparalleled and unforgettable page in the history of the United States. May their legends, both true and fictitious, live forever in the hearts of all Americans.

Chapter One

United States Marshal Clay Shannon was walking
in the garden of Rancho Alvarez, his wife Charlotte
beside him. The night was warm, the moon was full,
and the flowering bushes in the garden filled the air
with their perfume.

"Clay," Charlotte said, taking his arm, "you promised me that one day you'd tell me more about yourself . . . where you came from, who your family was,
and how you first became a lawman. Will you tell me
now?"

Shannon smiled at her. Charlotte Alvarez Shannon
was the last survivor of an old Spanish family that had
settled in New Mexico many generations before. She
and Shannon had fought side by side to save Charlotte's ranch, her family, and her town from the evil
that had threatened to destroy all of them. The battle
had been hard and costly, and by the time it was finally
won, Clay and Charlotte had discovered that there was

1

a bond between them that neither wanted to break. They had been married for just a month, and Shannon looked down at her now with pleasure and affection.

"Are you sure you want to know?" he asked. "All of it?"

Charlotte's expression was solemn, but her dark eyes flashed mischievously.

"Everything," she said. "The good and the bad. If there is any bad."

"Oh, yes," Shannon said wryly. "There's lots of that."

Charlotte led him to one of the garden's benches and sat down beside him.

"Tell me," she said. "Please."

"There's really not much to tell," he said thoughtfully. "I grew up in a little Kansas prairie town, a place called Dry Wells. It was like most of those dusty frontier settlements. One hotel, one saloon, a general store, a one-room school, and not much else. Just a few hundred people, scratching out a living as best they could. My father was the marshal there. I guess that's how it all began."

He paused, remembering.

Nineteen-year-old Clay Shannon latched the corral gate and then stood with his foot resting on the lowest of the wooden rails, looking thoughtfully at the horses milling about inside the fence. They were spirited animals, tossing their heads and snorting. Shannon enjoyed just watching them. He loved horses, and this was a good string, perhaps the best he'd ever had. It was time to sell some of them to bring in a little much-needed cash, but there was one he planned to keep for himself, a buckskin stallion he'd had his eye on. *Speed and heart,* Shannon thought. *A man could ride a long way on that one.*

He hung his lariat over a fencepost and headed for the house. As he climbed the steps his father came out of the door, buckling on his gunbelt as he crossed the porch. The star on the older man's shirt gleamed dully in the late afternoon sunlight.

"Hi, Dad," Shannon said. "Sorry I'm late. Hope I didn't miss dinner."

"Don't worry," his father said. "Cook saved some for you. I'm going back to the office for awhile. Got some paperwork to finish. What are you up to this evening?"

"Thought I'd do a little studying," Shannon said.

"I'll see you later then," the elder Shannon said. He walked away into the gathering twilight.

Shannon ate his supper in the kitchen, a heavy book open on the table before him. The woman who cooked for Marshal Dan Shannon and his son had gone home and the house was quiet, which was the way the younger Shannon liked it. He was studying law under the tutelage of the town's one and only attorney, and there was much to learn. Shannon found himself deeply interested in the law, with all of its wisdom and all of its failings, and somehow he knew that it would, inevitably, be his life.

He had been reading through the law book for nearly an hour when he was suddenly distracted from his studies by the sound of running feet crossing the front porch.

"Clay!" someone shouted, pounding on the door. "Clay, are you in there?"

Shannon hurried to the door and opened it. Ed Miles, the storekeeper, was standing there, his thinning hair tousled and his eyes wide with shock.

"Hello, Mr. Miles," Shannon said. "What's wrong?"

"It's your father," Miles said breathlessly. "He's been shot."

A cold chill ran through Shannon's body.

"How badly is he hurt?" he asked, dreading the answer.

"I don't know, Clay," Miles replied. "They took him over to Doc Carson's. Doc sent me to get you."

Shannon pushed past the storekeeper and ran headlong down the street. Miles followed some distance behind him.

The office of Dr. Amos Carson stood halfway along the main street, a shabby board building like most of the structures in the town. The physician was standing in the open doorway, leaning against the doorframe. He looked tired.

"Doc!" Shannon cried as he vaulted up the steps of the boardwalk. "How's my father? Is it bad?"

Carson rubbed his eyes.

"Your father's dead, Clay," he said. "He was dead when they brought him in. I'm sorry, boy. I'm truly sorry."

Shannon could only stare at him, completely stunned.

"I want to see him," he said in a strangled voice. "Where is he?"

The doctor took him into the office. The body of

Marshal Daniel Shannon lay upon the examination table. His shirt was stained with blood. So was his badge.

The storekeeper arrived, followed closely by the town's mayor. Mayor Partridge was a corpulent man with a high-pitched voice and red face. He was the town's banker when not performing his mayoral duties.

"How's the marshal?" he said, blinking in the lamplight.

"How does he look?" Doc Carson snapped, waving a hand at the still form on the table. "He's dead. That's how he is."

Clay Shannon tore his eyes away from his father's corpse and looked at Carson.

"What happened?" he asked. The shock was wearing off now, and rage was beginning to take its place. Ed Miles pushed forward through the gathering crowd.

"I saw it all, Clay," he said. "It happened right in my store. It was that no-good Pete Catlett who did it. He came in drunk and wanted to buy some supplies on credit. The Catlett family never paid a bill in their lives, and I told Pete he'd have to pay cash. He got mad and started tearing up the place, knocking things over and pulling stuff off the shelves. Then he drew his gun and started waving it around. I was afraid of what he might do next, so I sent my boy to get the marshal."

"And then?" Shannon asked, already guessing what had followed.

"Your dad came right away," Miles said. "He told Catlett to calm down, and then asked for his gun.

Catlett held out his pistol butt-first, like he was going to give it up, but when your dad reached for it, Catlett spun the gun around and shot him point-blank in the chest."

The storekeeper looked wide-eyed at Mayor Partridge.

"The marshal never had a chance, Mayor," he said. He never even drew his gun."

"Didn't anybody try to help Dad?" Shannon asked angrily, looking around at the people in the room.

"Of course nobody tried to help him," Doc Carson replied bitterly. "No one in this flea-bitten town has enough guts to defend themselves or anybody else. That's why they hired your father to be the marshal."

Clay Shannon looked down at the stained badge on his father's chest.

Fifty dollars a month, he thought. *That's all Dad got for wearing that badge. And not a single deputy to back him up, because the town didn't want to pay for one. Fifty dollars a month, and now he's gone, shot down for no reason by a drunken hoodlum in a pointless brawl.*

"Where's Catlett now?" he asked. "Still in the store?"

"Naw, he's in my place now," a voice behind them said. Joe Pitts, the owner of the saloon, had entered the doctor's office while they were talking. "He was drunk when he came in," Pitts said, "and he's getting drunker by the minute. Somebody better do something before he starts wrecking the joint."

"But what can we do?" the mayor said. "Catlett's a braggart and a bully, but he's good with a gun and with the marshal dead, nobody around here could take him."

"Nobody around here would even try," the doctor said acidly.

"I will," Clay Shannon said.

He carefully unpinned the badge from his father's shirt.

"Mayor," he said, "swear me in. I'll get Catlett."

"You?" the doctor said, raising his eyebrows. "You're too young to take on a thug like Catlett. He'll eat you alive."

Shannon unbuckled his father's gunbelt and swung it around his own waist.

"Swear me in," he said, his eyes hard.

"Not a chance, boy," Mayor Partridge said. "I don't want any more trouble."

"You're going to have more trouble anyway if you don't act quickly," Shannon said, buckling the gunbelt.

"Go ahead, Mayor," the saloon keeper said. "What have you got to lose?"

"Yes," Shannon said bitterly. "What have you got to lose? You don't even have to pay me."

"Oh, all right," Mayor Partridge said petulantly. "I guess we've got to take the chance. But no more shooting. Just arrest Catlett. Don't kill him."

"That's up to Catlett," Shannon said, pushing his way out of the room.

Shannon left the doctor's office and stepped off the boardwalk into the dust of the street. His father's star was pinned securely to his shirt. He had not wiped off the bloodstains.

Even as he was crossing the street, he could hear

Catlett cursing drunkenly in the saloon. Shannon drew the heavy six-gun from its holster and cocked the hammer. Then he cautiously approached the swinging doors of the saloon and looked inside. Catlett was at the bar, raising a shot glass to his lips. He downed the whiskey and wiped his mouth with his sleeve.

"Gimme 'nother drink," he said to the bartender. "An' leave the bottle."

He started to fill the shot glass again. Clay Shannon pushed open the swinging doors and walked across the room toward the bar, the cocked six-gun held close to his side. Catlett raised the glass to his lips and then paused as he caught sight of Shannon out of the corner of his eye.

"Catlett," Shannon said, raising the pistol, "you're under arrest."

Pete Catlett put down the glass, leaned against the bar, and faced Shannon.

"Who're you?" he asked thickly. "I don't know you."

"I'm the son of the man you gunned down in the general store a half-hour ago," Shannon replied. "Or don't you remember that?"

Catlett's face twisted in derision as he saw the badge on Shannon's shirt. "Well, well," he said with a sneer. "Another law dog. Or maybe I should say 'law puppy.' You ain't old enough to be a marshal, sonny."

"I'm old enough to take in a whiskey-soaked coward like you," Shannon said. "You're going to jail, Catlett. Now hand over the six-gun. Do it very slowly, and don't try that fancy road-agent spin you used on my father."

"Why, sure, kid, I'll hand over my gun," Catlett said with a laugh. His hand darted toward his holster. "Nobody takes me to jail," he snarled, starting to draw.

Shannon pulled the trigger of his revolver. The explosion was deafening in the confines of the saloon, and powder smoke filled the room. Catlett dropped his gun and staggered back, clutching at his abdomen.

"You shot me!" he wailed. "You *shot* me!"

He collapsed onto the floor, groaning.

Shannon glanced around. Several men were standing in the doorway behind him, watching in fascination.

"Come on," Shannon said, "some of you people help me get this filth over to the jail."

They put Catlett on a bunk in one of the cells. He lay there moaning while Doc Carson inspected the wound.

"I'm dyin'," Catlett whimpered.

"Unfortunately," Carson said, "you're not. The bullet just glanced off your ribs. You'll live."

"Yes," Shannon said, watching from the cell doorway. "He'll live. Live to hang."

When he had locked Pete Catlett up for the night, Shannon came out of the jail into the adjoining marshal's office. He hung the cell keys on their hook and looked around. He had been in the office often when his father was alive. Now, as the reality of his father's death began to sink in, it was as if he was seeing it for the first time.

The mayor, the doctor, the saloon owner, and the storekeeper were all gathered in the room.

"Well," the saloon owner said, "that's that. Good work, Clay."

The mayor bit his lip. He looked worried.

"That's *not* that, not by a long shot," he said. "We've got Pete Catlett, but he has two brothers who are just as wild as he is, and Old Man Catlett is the worst of all. When he hears we've shot one of his sons and tossed him in jail, the whole clan will come into town fighting mad."

"Maybe we should form a vigilance committee," the storekeeper said nervously. "Be ready for them."

"And get ourselves killed?" the mayor asked, his voice rising an octave at the thought of it. "We're not gunfighters. People like the Catletts are the marshal's job."

"Yeah," the saloon owner said, "but we don't have a marshal anymore, remember? We got to find somebody else, and fast."

Clay Shannon took off his father's badge, placed it carefully on the desk, and started toward the door. The anger that had carried him through the confrontation in the saloon was beginning to subside, and the inevitable reaction was setting in. He felt ill, and he wanted to escape from the stuffy, crowded office and breathe the cool night air for a few moments before facing the sad task that now lay ahead of him.

"Hold it, Clay," the mayor said. "Where are you going?"

"To the undertaker's," Shannon said. "I've got to make arrangements for my father's funeral."

"Wait a minute," the mayor said, mopping his forehead with his handkerchief. "Joe here is right. With your dad gone, we need someone to replace him, and you did fine in the saloon tonight. How would you like to keep that badge for awhile?"

"No thanks," Shannon said. "I got the man who killed my father. That's all I wanted."

"But we need you, boy," the mayor said. "Put that star back on. Be the town marshal. You can follow right in your dad's footsteps."

"Follow where?" the doctor said with a growl. "To Boot Hill?"

"Stay out of this, Doc," the mayor said. "Come on, Clay, keep the badge. We'll pay you fifty dollars a month, just like your dad."

"Not interested," Shannon said firmly. "I've seen what fifty dollars a month bought him."

"But Clay," the mayor pleaded, "you've got an obligation to this town. After all, you're the one who shot Pete Catlett. The rest of the Catletts will want revenge. They'll come storming into town, and who knows what they'll do when they get here? You can't run out on us now."

Shannon frowned. He did not like the idea of running out on anything.

The mayor sensed imminent victory.

"We need you, son," he said with an oily smile. "We really *need* you."

Shannon hesitated a moment longer, then went back to the desk and picked up the badge.

"All right," he said, "but only until this mess with the Catletts is over. Meanwhile, I've got to go bury my father."

Chapter Two

They buried him the next morning. The cemetery stood on the edge of town, dusty and neglected. In Dry Wells, as in most frontier settlements, death came often and few bothered to remember those who had died. On this day, however, many of the townspeople had turned out to attend the funeral, for the elder Shannon had been well–liked. The community had no minister, so the mourners murmured the Lord's Prayer and sang a hymn, and Mayor Partridge delivered a long speech about how the departed Marshal Shannon had served his neighbors well and faithfully for many years, and died bravely defending them.

Shannon was standing at the front of the crowd, but he hardly heard the Mayor's flowery words. He was gazing blindly out across the empty prairie, still trying to make sense of the sudden and violent events that had brought his world crashing down around him.

After the mourners had departed, Shannon lingered

behind, watching as the gravediggers shoveled dirt onto the coffin. When they had finished and left, he stood at the edge of the grave for a long time, staring down at it. Shannon's mother had died years previously, and he had no brothers or sisters. Now his father too was gone. Memories of the past tore at Shannon's heart as he stood there, bare-headed, beside the mound of earth that was all that remained of his childhood.

At last, reluctantly, he turned away and walked slowly back into town, feeling for the first time the loneliness of those whose loved ones have left them behind forever.

Doc Carson found him an hour later, sitting on the boardwalk in front of the marshal's office, cleaning his father's six-gun. The pieces of the disassembled weapon were spread out upon a little table beside Shannon's chair, and Carson noted with approval that another revolver, fully loaded, lay on the tabletop within easy reach of Shannon's hand.

"Are you all right, Clay?" the doctor asked, seeing Shannon's haggard features and the dark circles under his eyes.

"No," said Shannon. "I'm not."

The doctor nodded. He knew that Shannon and his father had been very close.

"Don't do it, Clay," he said.

"Don't do what?"

"Don't try to play marshal. It's too dangerous. That badge on your shirt is nothing but a nice shiny target for anybody looking for trouble, and you just don't have the experience or the skills for the job."

"I was good enough to get Pete Catlett."

"He was drunk, and you were lucky. Next time it won't be so easy. In a few days, when they hear about this, Old Man Catlett and his other sons will come charging in here to break Pete out of jail. The old man's a whole lot smarter than Pete, and his two brothers are a whole lot tougher. If you go up against them wearing that badge, they'll blow your head off."

Shannon shrugged.

"They might do it anyway, with or without the badge."

"Then leave Dry Wells now. You don't owe this town anything, despite what our esteemed mayor told you last night. There's nothing to hold you here. You've got no family anymore, and that little place of your dad's was only rented. Ride out, Clay, while you still can."

Shannon finished reassembling the six-gun, loaded it, and slid it back into his holster.

"Doc," he said, "my father and I talked often about what it means to be a lawman. He told me many times that anyone who carries a star must always act with courage and integrity, and that he must never forget his obligation to the people who depend on him. He believed that, very deeply. Well, I'm wearing his star now, and I'm going to try very hard to be the kind of lawman he would have wanted me to be."

"Courage and integrity can't beat a fast draw, son," the doctor said quietly.

"Perhaps not," Shannon said, "but Mayor Partridge was right about one thing. When the Catletts get here, they might not stop with just breaking Pete out and killing me. They might decide to wreck the town out of spite, and then a lot of people would get hurt. No, Doc, I took this job, and I won't back out of it now. I have to see it through, one way or another."

"Where's that lawyer you've been studying with?" Carson asked. "You ought to talk to him about this."

"He's over at the county seat, trying a court case," Shannon replied. "He probably won't be back for several more days. Anyway, it wouldn't matter what he said. I've made up my mind."

Carson rolled his eyes in frustration.

"Don't be a fool, boy," he said. "Ride out."

"I can't, Doc."

"Well, then," the doctor said grimly, "you'd better learn to use that six-gun *muy pronto*, because otherwise the only kind of lawman you're going to be is a dead one."

A mile east of town, Shannon turned the buckskin through the gate of a small ranch house nestled in a grove of trees. As he dismounted in front of the house, a middle-aged woman came out of the door and stood on the porch, shading her eyes with her hand against the glare.

"Oh, hello, Clay," she said. "What brings you out this way?"

"I need to talk with Mr. Lane," Shannon said.

"I guess it'll be all right," said the woman, who was Lane's widowed daughter. "Dad's inside. Come on in. But please don't stay too long. He gets tired rather easily."

Tom Lane was sitting in an easy chair in the ranch

house's front room. He was an elderly man with a weathered face and piercing blue eyes. His right leg was extended stiffly out in front of him, and a cane rested against the arm of the chair. In his younger days, Lane had been a lawman in several frontier towns, earning himself a reputation for honesty and a fast gun. He had served as the marshal of Dry Wells for many years until he had gotten into a shootout with a band of outlaws intent on robbing the town's one and only bank. The surviving bank robbers rode out of town with the money, leaving Marshal Lane lying in the dust with a shattered knee cap. The bank eventually reopened, but Tom Lane's career as a lawman was over. Shannon's father had replaced him as town marshal.

As Shannon entered, Lane got stiffly to his feet and extended his hand.

"I heard about your dad, Clay," he said. "I'm truly sorry. He was a good man, a very good man. I see you're wearing his star."

"Yes, they hired me to take his place. Or at least to take his job."

"Why?" Lane asked, resuming his seat.

"The mayor thinks the Catletts will shoot up the town and break Pete Catlett out of jail," Shannon replied as he sat down.

"They probably will," Lane said. "That's a rough outfit. Old Man Catlett is as mean as they come, and he'll be boiling mad when he hears about what you did to his worthless son. Does the town really expect you to stand up to the whole Catlett family?"

"Yes. Funny, isn't it?"

"It's not funny at all," Lane said. "They'll chew you up and spit you out, son. You haven't got a prayer."

Shannon shrugged.

"I'm the town marshal now," he said. "I have to try."

"I see. Well, suppose you win the fight with the Catletts. What then?"

"I may keep the star," Shannon said. "Dad was a good marshal. Maybe in time I can be like him."

Lane's brow furrowed.

"Look, Clay," he said, "I was your father's friend, and I know he wouldn't want you to be a lawman. His dream was to see you become a lawyer or a judge, to make something of yourself. He told me once that the last thing he wanted you to do was to wind up like him, wearing a tin star and risking your life every day, year in and year out, for a few measly dollars."

"I know he felt that way," Clay said, "but perhaps he was wrong. Perhaps I was meant to be a lawman too. I might even get to like it."

Lane laughed harshly.

"That's the problem, Clay. With some men, once they carry the star it gets in their blood and they can never stop. Believe me, I know. After awhile, even if you want to quit you can't, because it's become your whole life. But it's a hard life, and an unprofitable one. You get no thanks from those you serve, and if you're honest you die broke in a shabby rented room in some one-horse town in the middle of nowhere. I wore a badge for twenty-five years, and what did it get me? A game leg and a lot of bad memories. Take off the badge, Clay. Get out of Dry Wells. Go somewhere else and start a new life. That's what your father would have advised you to do."

"I can't quit," Shannon said doggedly. "Not until this Catlett business is settled."

Lane shook his head in exasperation.

"You're as stubborn as your father," he said. "Well, you've made your decision, and it's time to think about the consequences of it. Are you any good with that six-gun?"

"That's what I came to talk to you about. I need you to teach me."

"There isn't enough time, Clay. Skill with a six-gun isn't something you acquire overnight. Right now Old Man Catlett and his whelps are probably off somewhere rustling somebody's cattle, but in a day or two they're going to hear what happened yesterday evening, and they'll be here long before you can learn to be a gunfighter."

"I know that," Shannon said, "but anything I could learn from you—even just one small thing—might make the difference. Will you show me as much as you can in the time we have?"

Tom Lane hesitated. He knew that this was not what Dan Shannon would have wished for his son. But Lane also knew that if Clay stubbornly insisted on walking into a gunfight, then for his old friend's sake he could hardly refuse to try to help him survive it.

"You won't give up this idea of facing the Catletts?" Lane asked.

"No," Shannon said firmly. "I have to do it, with or without your help."

With a sigh, Lane reached for his cane and began the painful process of rising from his chair.

"All right, son," he said. "There's a box of .45 shells in the top drawer of the chest over there. Get 'em, and we'll go out back and see what can be done."

He limped toward the rear of the ranch house, with Shannon right behind him.

"Where are you going, Dad?" his daughter called from the kitchen.

"Clay and I are going to do a little shooting," Lane said.

"Well, don't stay on your feet too long. You know what the doctor said."

"I'll be fine, Martha," Lane said patiently. "Don't worry."

They walked some distance away from the house and stopped a few yards from a barbed wire fence. Beyond the fence, the open prairie stretched emptily as far as the eye could see.

"Have you had much practice with the six-gun?" Lane asked.

"Some," Shannon said. "Dad and I used to go out shooting at tin cans once in a while. It was mostly just for fun, though. He never talked much about gunfighting."

"That's because he didn't want you to be a gunfighter," Lane said. "Well, there are some things you need to know, so let's get at it."

He showed Shannon how to position his gunbelt so that the six-gun came easily to his hand, and how to cock the weapon as he brought it up out of his holster. They talked about the importance of balance in a six-gun, and Lane showed Shannon how to use the point-ing qualities of a well-balanced weapon to bring the muzzle effortlessly onto the target.

"Above all, Clay," Lane said, "remember that it's not enough just to be fast. Accuracy is more important than speed. When the shooting starts, take that extra split second and be sure you hit what you're aiming at. I've seen men blaze away at each other a dozen feet apart and miss every time. You can't afford to do that if you're a lawman. No matter how fast your draw is, if you can't shoot straight you'll wind up dead sooner or later. Probably sooner."

He leaned on his cane.

"Now," he said, "let's see what you can do."

"What should I fire at?"

"Try that old fencepost over there. Our hired hand's going to be replacing it pretty soon anyway, so it won't matter if we chew it up a bit. Go ahead."

In one quick motion Shannon drew the six-gun and fired. Splinters flew from the post, chest high.

Lane's eyebrows went up.

"Do that again," he said. "Fire twice this time."

Two more chunks of wood flew from the post. Lane looked consideringly at Shannon.

"You're fast, son," he said. "Fast *and* accurate. I'm impressed."

"Thanks, Mr. Lane," Shannon said, reloading the six-gun and sliding it back into its holster, "but what can I do to get better?"

"Practice, my boy. Practice every chance you get, from now until. . . . well, as long as you can. Come on, let's get back to the house. This bum leg's acting up, and there are some other things I want to tell you."

They returned to the ranch house and Lane once more eased himself into his chair. His daughter Martha hovered around him, adjusting the cushions and scolding him for being outside so long.

"Martha," Lane said with a wink at Shannon, "stop acting like a mother hen and get us some coffee."

When they were sipping the coffee and Martha had returned to the kitchen, Lane looked quizzically at Shannon.

"Clay," he said, "they say free advice is worth what you pay for it, and I've already given you a lot of it. Think you can stand some more?"

"I'd appreciate anything you can tell me, Mr. Lane," Shannon said. He knew that to him at this moment, advice from Tom Lane was worth its weight in gold.

"Very well," Lane said, leaning forward and looking intently into Shannon's eyes. "There are certain rules a lawman has to remember if he wants to survive, and I want you to learn them by heart. Rule Number One is *always expect the unexpected*. Your father forgot that rule. That's why he's dead. I'm sorry to put it so harshly, son, but it's true."

"I realize that," Shannon said. "I won't forget. What's the second rule?"

"Just this. *If you have to use your gun, shoot to kill, because the other man will be trying to kill you.* All this nonsense about shooting a gun out of somebody's hand is just that. Nonsense. Don't try. There's no time for charity in a gun fight."

"And Rule Number Three?"

"Number Three is to *always take advantage of any edge the situation offers you.* For example, the sun and the wind can be your allies. Let them help you. Whenever possible, fight with the sun at your back, because then it will be in your opponents' eyes. The same with the wind. Keep your back to it, so that it will blow dust in their faces, not yours. Another thing is, if the circumstances permit it, try to come up behind them. The element of surprise is often your best weapon."

"I'll remember," Shannon said.

Lane shifted his bad leg, grimacing in pain as he moved it. Seeing his discomfort, Shannon rose from his chair.

"Thanks, Mr. Lane," he said. "I appreciate your help."

Lane held up his hand.

"Wait," he said. "I'm not finished. There's something else you need to know. There's a fourth rule, an important one. It says that you should never fight a battle you can't win. You can afford to buck the odds at a faro table, because then you're only risking money. When you buck the odds in a gunfight, you're risking your life. Don't do it. If you're overmatched, back down."

Shannon shook his head.

"Lawmen can't do that," he said.

"Sure they can," Lane said. "Plenty of them have."

"Well, *I* can't," Shannon said.

"No," Lane said sadly, "I don't suppose you can."

The old marshal paused, weighing his next words.

"One final thing, Clay," he said. "Don't underestimate the Catletts. They're ugly and dirty and usually drunk, but they're dangerous, too. Among other things, they don't care how they make a dollar. That so-called ranch of theirs up north always seems to have a lot of cattle on it that belong to somebody else. Most of their riders are one jump ahead of the law, and all of the brothers have hired out their guns from time to time."

"Nice people," Shannon said with a little smile.

"They'd cut a man's throat for the change in his pockets," Lane said. "Your father wasn't the first one they've killed, and he probably won't be the last. So be careful, Clay. Don't let yourself become another notch on one of the Catletts' guns."

Shannon reached out and shook Lane's hand again.

"Thanks for the advice, Mr. Lane," he said.

"You can thank me by staying alive," Lane said. "Good luck, son."

Lane hobbled to the door with Shannon and then stood there, resting on his cane. He watched thoughtfully as Shannon rode away, back toward town.

Lane's daughter came up behind him.

"What's wrong with that boy?" she asked, wiping her hands on her apron. "He sounded so serious."

"He's not a boy anymore, Martha," Lane said bleakly. "He stopped being a boy last night, when he put on that star he's wearing."

Chapter Three

The next day dawned bright and clear. Clay Shannon unlocked the marshal's office and went in. The old man who watched the jail when there was a prisoner in the cells had been sleeping on the bunk in the corner. He sat up as Shannon came in.

"Morning, Ben," Shannon said. "Everything quiet?"

"Sure," said the old man, rubbing his eyes. "Nice and peaceful."

"Hey!" a voice cried from the jail. "When do I get some breakfast?"

Shannon went into the jail. Pete Catlett was standing at the front of his cell, gripping the bars and looking surly.

"That's enough out of you, Catlett," Shannon said. "Open your mouth again and I'll shove a boot down your throat."

"That ain't no way to treat a prisoner," Catlett grumbled.

24

"It's a good way to treat a murderer," Shannon said. "Get back on that bunk. Ben will bring your breakfast over from the restaurant in a little while, and Doc Carson will stop by to check your bandage. Meanwhile, just keep quiet. You're lucky I didn't kill you last night. I may still do it if you give me any trouble."

Catlett opened his mouth to protest, then thought better of it. The look in Shannon's eyes had told him that the new marshal of Dry Wells wasn't joking.

The jailer left to get his own breakfast, and Shannon sat down at the desk. He began looking absently through the wanted posters he had found in one of the drawers, but his mind was elsewhere. *It's been two days now,* he thought. *The rest of the Catletts ought to be along soon. What will I do when they get here? How will I deal with them?*

The jailer returned, wearing the remnants of his scrambled eggs on his shirt and bearing a tray with the prisoner's breakfast on it. Shannon took the food into the jail, shoved the tray unceremoniously under the cell door, and then came back into the office.

"I'm going to get some breakfast myself, Ben," he said, "and then take a turn around the town. Come and get me if anything happens."

The sun was halfway to the zenith when Shannon returned to the office. He barred the door behind him and sat down at the desk. Old Ben was moving about in the jail, sweeping it out as he had every morning since Shannon's father had hired him.

There was a sudden commotion in the street, and

Shannon heard horses pulling up in front of the office. Instinctively he drew his gun and started for the door.

"You in the jail!" a gravelly voice shouted. "Open up!"

Old Ben went to the office's open window.

"It's the Catletts, Clay," he said. "Old Man Catlett and Pete's two brothers, Frank and Al."

Clay moved over beside the window and looked cautiously out. Three rough-looking horsemen were sitting astride their mounts directly in front of the office steps. One was a tall, gray-haired man, the other two shorter and younger. They all had sour looks on their faces, and they were all carrying repeating rifles. Shannon swallowed hard. Three to one. Well, he had known this would happen sooner or later. He'd accepted the badge, and he had to accept the risks that came with it. *I suppose it could have been worse,* he told himself. *At least they didn't bring their whole gang with them.*

"What do you want?" Clay called through the window, knowing full well what they wanted.

"I want my boy," Old Man Catlett replied. "You get him out here right now or we're coming in to get him."

"He's under arrest for murder," Shannon said. "I can't let him out. You know that."

"Yeah," Old Man Catlett shouted, "and you know what we're gonna do to you if we have to bust in there."

All three of the Catletts climbed down out of their saddles and stepped up onto the boardwalk, holding their rifles at the ready.

Shannon's mind was racing. The office door was

flimsy, and three men would have little difficulty breaking it down with rifle butts. Something had to be done, and time was short. He went over to the gun rack on the far wall, unlocked the chain that secured the guns, and took down a double-barreled shotgun. The shells for the shotgun were kept in the bottom drawer of the desk, and Shannon picked up a handful. He shoved two of them into the chambers of the shotgun, then stuffed the rest into his pocket.

"Unlock the back door for me, will you Ben?" he asked. "Do it quietly, and then lock it again after I'm outside."

"Doggonit, Clay," Ben said, "you ain't goin' out there by yourself, are you?"

"I don't have much choice," Shannon replied, closing the breech of the shotgun.

"You want me to go with you?" the jailer asked. "I ain't afraid of them Catletts."

"No thanks, Ben," Shannon said. "I appreciate it—I really do—but I need you to stay in here and watch Pete." He tossed the jailer one of the other shotguns. "Here," he said. "Load this. If the Catletts break in, fire both barrels and then take off out the back door before the smoke clears."

"But what about Pete?"

Shannon cocked the hammers of his shotgun.

"If they get by me," he said, "let them have Pete. He isn't worth dying for."

Grumbling unhappily, Ben held the back door open while Shannon went through it. Shannon waited beside the door until he heard Ben softly turn the key behind him, then slipped as silently as possible along the back wall of the jail. At the rear corner, he peered cautiously up the little alleyway that separated the jail from the nearby buildings. Seeing no one, he began to move up the alley, the shotgun held before him. At the mouth of the alleyway he stopped and carefully looked around the corner toward the front door of the office. The Catletts were all standing near the door, watching it intently.

"Come on," Old Man Catlett shouted, "open up! You got one minute, and then we're coming in shooting."

Shannon ducked back against the side wall of the building, gathering himself for what he had to do next. As he hefted the six-gun in its holster to make certain it was free, he discovered that his hands were sweating. He hastily wiped them on his shirt. *You don't have time to be afraid now,* he told himself. *Perhaps later. If there is a later.* Then he took a deep breath and marched boldly around the corner, stepped up onto the boardwalk, and pointed the cocked shotgun directly at the three men standing outside the office door.

Caught unaware, the Catletts gaped at him for a moment, then started to swing their rifles toward him.

"Hold it!" Shannon barked. "The first man who moves gets a load of buckshot in the belly!"

The startled Catletts froze, staring wide-eyed at the double-barreled shotgun that was centered on them waist-high.

"Now drop those rifles," Shannon said. The Catletts hesitated. The two sons looked questioningly at their father.

"What'll we do, Pa?" one of them asked plaintively.

"Play it smart, Mr. Catlett," Shannon said. "Drop the rifles, or you'll be the first to die."

Old Man Catlett uttered a string of filthy curses. His eyes were fixed on Shannon and full of hate. Then he looked again at the menacing shotgun muzzles.

"Awright," he said. "He's got the drop on us. Put down them rifles."

"Now unbuckle your gunbelts," Shannon said, "and let them fall. Do it nice and easy, so I don't get nervous and accidentally pull these triggers."

Fuming with anger, the Catletts took off their gunbelts and deposited them on the boardwalk. As they did so, the front door of the office opened and old Ben appeared, holding his shotgun.

"Now," Shannon said to the Catletts, "you men back up one step and then stand as still as statues. Ben, pick up their rifles and gunbelts and toss them into the office."

As Shannon waited for Ben to collect the weapons, he became aware that people were now creeping out of the adjoining buildings to see what was happening.

"You folks stay back," Shannon shouted at them. "If I have to shoot these skunks, I don't want any of you getting hurt."

The onlookers scuttled for cover, but continued to watch expectantly from windows and doorways.

Waiting for the killing to begin, I suppose, Shannon thought to himself.

"Now listen to me, Mr. Catlett," he said, "and listen carefully, because I'm only going to say this once. Your son shot my father in cold blood. He's under arrest for murder, and he's going to stand trial for it.

If you try to interfere, you'll be sitting in a jail cell too."

"Big talk," Old Man Catlett said with a sneer. "We can take a cub like you anytime we want to."

"You'd better quit while you're ahead, Mr. Catlett," Shannon replied. "Up to now no harm's been done here today, so I'm going to let all of you ride out the way you came in. But if I ever see you anywhere near this jail again, or if you ever start any trouble of any kind in this town, I'll personally hand you a one-way ticket to Boot Hill. Understand?"

"We'll get you for this," Frank Catlett said with a growl. "You can count on it."

"Get on your horses, all of you," Shannon said. "I'm through talking."

"What about our guns?" Frank's brother Al asked sulkily.

"I'll keep them for souvenirs," Shannon said. "Now head out, and don't look back. Go on, *move!*"

Blaspheming fiercely, the Catletts caught up the reins of their horses and mounted. As Old Man Catlett settled himself in his saddle, he cast one last male-volent look at Shannon.

"You're dead, Shannon," he said. "You hear me? Dead."

"Good-bye, Mr. Catlett," Shannon said. "Nice knowing you."

Sullenly, the Catletts turned their horses and rode slowly out of town, looking neither to the left or the right. In a few minutes they had vanished into the haze of the day.

When they were out of sight, Shannon took another

deep breath and exhaled slowly. Then he uncocked the shotgun and set it down against the front wall of the office. He felt suddenly weak in the knees, so he leaned against the wall beside the shotgun, his mind a whirl.

Old Ben came back out of the office, a broad grin on his stubbled face.

"Son," he said with a chortle, "your dad would be proud of you. You handled them sidewinders like they was little kids sucking on their thumbs. I ain't seen the like in all my life."

"Thanks, Ben," Shannon said. "Thanks for backing me up, too."

People were now rushing toward Shannon, slapping him on the back, congratulating him. The mayor arrived, wiping his face with his handkerchief.

"Excellent, my boy, excellent!" he said. "Couldn't have done better myself."

Eventually the compliments petered out, and the crowd began to drift away. Doc Carson stayed behind, looking at Shannon with a pensive expression on his face.

"You should have killed them, Clay," he said. "You humiliated them, and they won't rest until they've gotten even."

"It wasn't necessary to kill them," Shannon said wearily.

"Yes it was," Carson said. "You just don't know it yet. You're not hard enough to be a lawman, Clay. You're just not hard enough. You believe too much in honor and fair play and mercy for those that don't deserve it. That's a serious fault in a gunfighter, and if you're not careful it's going to get you killed one day."

"Thanks for the kind words, Doc," Shannon said sarcastically. He picked up the shotgun and went into the office. There he returned the shotgun to the rack, sat down at the desk, and began to tremble violently.

Chapter Four

Early afternoon found Shannon saddling his horse in front of the jail. Another horse, already saddled, stood at the hitchrail nearby. Doc Carson came out of his office, saw what Shannon was doing, and walked across the street to greet him.

"Afternoon, Clay," he said. "What's all this?"

"I'm taking Pete Catlett to the county seat," Shannon replied.

"Why are you doing that?" Carson asked. "The U.S. Marshal is due through here in a few days. Transporting prisoners is his business. Let him take care of it."

"I want Catlett out of here before his relatives get up the courage to come back for him," Shannon said. "The next time I might not be able to hold them off. Don't worry, Doc. I'll be all right."

"I wish I could be sure of that," Carson said. "Why

33

not wait until morning? You shouldn't be spending a night on the trail alone with a killer."

"This won't wait until morning," Shannon said. "I want to get him out of town now, before something else happens."

"Then at least take somebody with you."

"No," Shannon said, "I don't want anybody else risking his neck. This is my responsibility."

He slung the saddlebags over the buckskin's back and slid his rifle into its scabbard.

"I'd better get moving," he said. "Excuse me while I go collect the guest of honor."

He came back out of the office a moment later pushing Pete Catlett ahead of him. Catlett was handcuffed, and he did not look pleased.

"What're you doin'?" he said angrily. "I'm wounded. I can't travel yet. The wound will bust open. I'll bleed to death."

"You have my deepest sympathy," Shannon said, shoving him over to the waiting horse.

"This isn't a good idea, Clay," Doc Carson said. "Please let somebody else do it."

"You better listen to the Doc, kid," Catlett said with a hiss, his pig eyes blazing. "I'll jump you the first chance I get and break your fool neck."

Shannon drew his six-gun, cocked it, and shoved it up under Catlett's chin.

"No you won't," he said, "because the moment you so much as twitch, I'll splatter your head all over the trail and leave you for the buzzards."

Doc Carson laughed.

"You're learning, son," he said. "You're learning."

Shannon removed the gun muzzle from Catlett's throat and stepped back.

"Now get up on the horse," he said, "and don't forget what I just told you."

"What about these bracelets?" Catlett demanded. "I can't ride no horse wearin' handcuffs."

"Then you'll walk," Shannon said. "Take your choice."

Catlett cursed and lurched into the saddle, groaning loudly. Then he sat there, glowering at Shannon, holding the reins awkwardly in his manacled hands.

Shannon mounted the buckskin, still covering Catlett with his revolver, and smiled at the doctor.

"See you, Doc," he said.

"I certainly hope so," Carson said glumly.

The road to the county seat ran eastward from Dry Wells. The first few miles were through flat country, but then the land became more broken and more desolate. Bluffs and ravines soon dominated the landscape, and great boulders rose beside the trail, dwarfing the two riders as they passed.

As the sun began to set, Shannon turned the horses into a clear space between the rocks and reined up. He dismounted and waited for Catlett to climb down, covering him all the while with his six-gun.

"We stoppin' for the night?" Catlett demanded as he struggled out of the saddle.

"No," Shannon said. "We'll rest the horses for an hour and then move on."

"But I gotta stop," Catlett insisted. "My wound hurts. Let's stay here 'til mornin'."

"Get this straight, Catlett," Shannon said. "The only time we're going to stop between here and the county seat will be to give the horses a breather, so quit whining about it. Here's your dinner."

He reached into his saddlebags and pulled out some hard biscuits. He tossed one to Catlett, who caught it awkwardly with his manacled hands.

"Not much of a meal," he said dejectedly.

"I'll tell the chef you're unhappy with the menu," Shannon said, biting into his own biscuit.

"You gonna keep that six-gun pointed at me all the way to the county seat?" Catlett asked irritably.

"Yes," Shannon said. "I am."

An hour later they resumed the journey. Neither man spoke as they rode on through the night and into the early morning hours. Shannon kept the six-gun in his right hand the whole time, resting it against his thigh to ease the weight. Despite his best efforts, he soon found himself fighting to avoid falling asleep in the saddle. He knew he had to keep his mind clear for the job at hand, but by dawn he was barely awake, his mind dulled by weariness.

Just as the sky began to lighten in the east, they stopped again. As he was dismounting, Catlett seemed to lose his balance and half-fell off the horse, hitting the ground heavily. He howled in anguish and then began rolling around on the hard earth, moaning piteously.

"Hey, Marshal!" he said with a sob. "I've broke my arm! It's busted bad!"

Shannon moved closer to inspect the injury. Catlett did indeed appear to be holding his right arm at an awkward angle. His alertness blunted by his fatigue, Shannon fished in his pocket for the handcuff key, bent over the fallen man, and unlocked the cuff from Catlett's right wrist. With a maniacal roar, Catlett leaped up and charged at Shannon, striking him full in the midsection with a lowered shoulder. Shannon went over backwards, the breath momentarily knocked out of him by the stony ground and the impact of Catlett's body. As he struggled to sit up, he saw Catlett looming over him, outlined against the dawn. Catlett was raising a large rock over his head, his face twisted in rage.

"I told you I'd get you, Shannon!" he shrieked.

As Catlett brought the rock down on him, Shannon twisted away, desperately trying to evade the blow. The rock missed his skull and glanced off his left shoulder. Pain knifed through him, and he found himself wondering vaguely if his collarbone was broken.

But there was no time to think of that. Catlett was lunging at him again, cursing foully. Spittle was flying from his lips.

"Stop it!" Shannon shouted, leaping to his feet and raising the six-gun. "Don't make me shoot you!"

Catlett dodged away and ran toward Shannon's horse, the unlocked handcuffs swinging erratically from his left wrist. Still shouting obscenities, he yanked Shannon's rifle out of the saddle scabbard, jacked a round into the chamber, raised the weapon, and pulled the trigger. The bullet missed Shannon by half an inch.

"Drop the rifle, Catlett," Shannon said. "I'll kill you if I have to."

Catlett levered another round into the chamber of the rifle and again raised the weapon, aiming point-blank at Shannon's head. Shannon fired. Catlett screamed and dropped the rifle. He clutched at his midsection and staggered away a few steps. Then he fell forward on his face, rolled over, and lay still.

Shannon approached him warily, the six-gun cocked and ready. He saw immediately that there was no further danger. Catlett's eyes were now staring up at a sunrise he could no longer see.

Shannon stood silently looking down at the corpse, sickened by what he had just done. *I've killed a man,* he thought. *I've never killed anyone before. Now I'm a murderer, just like he was.* For a moment, self-disgust threatened to overwhelm him. Then he thought of his father, lying dead on Doc Carson's bloodstained examination table, cut down for no reason at all by this mad dog lying at his feet. Suddenly he seemed to hear a voice speaking to him as if from a great distance. *Clay,* said the voice, *he would have shot you if you hadn't fired first. You had no choice. If he had killed you and gotten away, sooner or later he would have killed others as well, innocent people you're sworn to protect. You did your duty as a lawman, son, and I'm truly proud of you.*

Shannon shook his head to clear it. *Now I'm imagining things,* he told himself. *Hearing voices in my head. I guess I must be pretty tired.*

He holstered his revolver and began the laborious job of getting the dead body onto Catlett's horse. His shoulder ached badly where the rock had struck it, but he ignored the pain as he lifted the body and heaved it over the saddle. The horse smelled blood and shied away nervously. Shannon calmed the animal, then finished tying the corpse to the horse's back so it would not slide off. Holding the other horse's reins, he remounted the buckskin and started back for Dry Wells, physically and mentally exhausted, but no longer troubled by regret.

Chapter Five

Shannon reached Dry Wells just before sunset, still leading the horse with Pete Catlett's body draped over its back. As Shannon moved slowly through town, people began following him, gesturing at the corpse as they talked excitedly among themselves. By the time Shannon reined up outside the undertaker's parlor, a sizeable crowd had gathered. The undertaker came out smiling, obviously pleased to have some additional business.

"Who is it, Clay?" he said, squinting nearsightedly at the body.

"Pete Catlett," Shannon said. "And he's all yours."

The onlookers began to buzz like bees among themselves.

"You hear that? It's Pete Catlett."

"Wonder who killed him?"

"The marshal, I reckon."

Shannon ignored all of this, but as he was untying

Catlett's body, he looked up and saw a roughly-dressed man who had been standing at the rear of the crowd walk rapidly away, untie his horse from a nearby hitchrail, and ride off at a fast trot.

Mayor Partridge came up, perspiring and out of breath.

"Who is *that*?" he asked, pointing a pudgy finger at the corpse.

"It's Pete Catlett, Mayor," the undertaker said.

Mayor Partridge's red face suddenly turned pale.

"What?" he cried. "Is he dead?"

"Yep," the undertaker said. "Looks good that way, don't he?"

"Who did it?" Partridge shouted. "I demand to know who did it!"

"I did," Shannon said.

"But you were supposed to take him to the county seat for trial. Why did you have to shoot him?"

"It seemed like a good idea at the time," Shannon said indifferently.

"But this is terrible!" Partridge exclaimed. "When Old Man Catlett hears about it, he'll tear Dry Wells apart!"

"In that case," Shannon said, glancing up the street at the rider who was now almost out of sight, "you'd better get ready, because I've got a hunch the Catletts are going to hear about it very soon."

The undertaker had stretched Pete Catlett's body out on a wooden plank, preparatory to carrying it into the undertaking parlor. Doc Carson arrived with his medical bag and knelt beside the dead man to examine him. At length he covered the corpse with the blanket the undertaker had provided, and stood up.

"In my professional opinion," he said, "this individual is totally, absolutely, and permanently dead. Anyone care to contest my diagnosis?"

"This is no time for humor, Doctor," Mayor Partridge said. "When word of this gets out, we may all be murdered in our beds."

"Oh, stop belly-aching, Elmer," Carson said to the mayor. "If it'll make you feel any better, I'll certify that Catlett died of natural causes."

Partridge blinked at the doctor in bewilderment.

"Natural causes?" he asked. "He died of *natural causes*?"

"Yes," Carson said solemnly. "Heart failure due to the presence of excessive lead in the bloodstream."

Partridge snorted and stamped away, muttering to himself.

The doctor had noticed that Shannon was favoring his left arm.

"What's wrong with the arm, Clay?" he asked.

"Nothing much, Doc," Shannon replied. "Just a sore shoulder, courtesy of our dead friend there."

"Let me take a look."

Shannon waved him away.

"That's not necessary, Doc," he said. "It's just a bruise. The only thing I need right now is some sleep." He elbowed his way through the gawking throng and departed, the buckskin horse plodding patiently behind him.

When he reached his house he rubbed down the buckskin, watered and fed him, and put him in the corral. Next he forked some hay into the corral for the other horses, and made sure their water trough was full. As he went about these chores, Shannon felt strangely detached, as if he were floating slowly through a very bad dream. When the animals had been cared for, he stumbled blindly into the empty house, fell upon his bed fully dressed, and was instantly asleep.

Chapter Six

Sunlight was flooding in through his bedroom window as Shannon awoke the next morning. He had slept around the clock, and the long slumber had left him groggy. In a few moments, however, his mind began to work again, and the harsh realization of what the day might bring came back to him with full force. Reluctantly, he rolled out of bed, made himself a pot of coffee, and then set out for the marshal's office. The people he encountered on the street pointedly looked the other way as he passed. *Nothing like having the support of your friends and neighbors,* Shannon thought to himself. *I'd be better off if I had leprosy.* He unlocked the door of the office and went in.

He checked all the weapons in the gun rack to make certain they were loaded, then decided to go across to the restaurant to get something to eat. However, when the food he had ordered was placed before him, he found that he was not really very hungry, and he picked at it without enthusiasm.

Nerves, he told himself. *That's another way of saying you're scared.*

He went back to the office and tried to distract himself by concentrating on a review of the wanted posters, but the ploy was unsuccessful. Questions kept running through his mind. *When will they come? How should I prepare? Where should I face them?*

Shortly before noon, he was startled to hear a voice calling him from the street.

"Marshal!" the voice shouted. "Hey, Marshal!"

Shannon went to the window and saw that a man he did not know was standing by the hitchrail. The man was short and swarthy, dressed in greasy buckskins and sporting a three-day growth of beard. Two guns were tied down to his thighs. As he waited, he was holding his hands high so that Shannon could see that they were empty.

Somebody's hired gun, Shannon thought. *Not hard to guess whose.*

"What do you want?" he asked.

"I'm not lookin' for any trouble, Marshal," the gunman replied. I just got a message for you."

Shannon opened the door and went out onto the boardwalk. He stopped there, his hand close to his six-gun, examining the stranger carefully and alert for any sudden hostile move.

"Well," he said, "what's the message?"

"Old Man Catlett sent me," the man said, grinning evilly. "Said to tell you he'll be ridin' in here tomorrow mornin' with his whole outfit. Said he's goin' to kill you, and if anyone else gets in his way, he'll burn this two-bit town right down to the ground."

"Nice of him to warn me," Shannon said.

"He wants you to sweat," the gunman said. "He likes to make people sweat."

"Fine," Shannon said. "Go back and tell him I'll be waiting for him. Then he can sweat a little too. Now get out of here."

The stranger mounted his horse and gave Shannon a malicious smile.

"See ya, Marshal," he said with a snicker. "Enjoy your last day."

"If Old Man Catlett rides in here shooting tomorrow," Shannon said, "it will be *his* last day. Tell him that, too."

"Oh, he ain't plannin' to shoot you, Marshal," the messenger said with an ugly laugh. "He's says he's goin' to come after you with a bullwhip and tear you to pieces with it. I seen him do that to a man once. It's a nasty way to die."

Still laughing, he spurred the horse forward and went away up the street at a gallop.

Several passersby had heard this exchange, and as Shannon re-entered his office he reflected that it probably would not be long before he received a visit from Mayor Partridge. True to this prediction, three and one-half minutes later Partridge came barging into the office, followed by members of the Dry Wells City Council.

"Shannon," Partridge bellowed, "what's all this about the Catlett gang burning the town?"

"They'll have to get past me first."

"But what if they do get past you? I must have been out of my mind to give you this job, Shannon. You can't stop those people. They'll trample all over you."

"Thanks for the vote of confidence."

"Don't you get smart-mouthed with me," Partridge said. "The townspeople are already upset by all this. When they hear about what that gunslinger said, they'll be frantic. And it's all your fault, Shannon. All your fault."

Doctor Carson had pushed his way through the door.

"If you're so alarmed about this, Elmer," he said, "why don't you do as Ed Miles suggested the other night? Form a vigilance committee. Meet the Catletts head on. They'll run if they see they're outnumbered."

"No!" the mayor shouted. "I said it then and I'm saying it now. I don't want any bloodbaths on the streets of Dry Wells. If we stay out of it, Catlett may ride off without doing anything to the town."

"After killing Clay, of course."

"Well, I can't help that. Shannon got us into this, and it's his duty to get us out of it."

"Nonsense," Doc Carson said. "You're acting like a total nitwit, Elmer, which is exactly what you are."

Partridge ignored this and waved his fist at Shannon.

"I hold you responsible for anything that happens here tomorrow, young man," he said. "If there's any killing or burning in Dry Wells, you'll answer to me."

"It's going to be pretty difficult for him to answer to you if he's dead," the doctor said with some asperity.

Partridge gave him a withering look and stalked out of the office. The City Council members hastily followed him.

"Isn't it grand, being a lawman?" Doc Carson said to Shannon. "Lots of danger, lots of criticism, and no gratitude whatsoever."

"Don't blame them, Doc," Shannon said. "They're just frightened."

"They're an ungrateful pack of yellow-bellied idiots," the doctor said, "and don't you forget it."

It was mid-afternoon when Shannon heard a wagon pulling up in front of the office. He went outside and discovered that it was Tom Lane's buckboard. Lane's daughter had the reins, while Lane himself sat stiffly on the seat beside her.

"Hello, Clay," Lane said as Shannon came out of the door. "Glad you're back safely."

"Didn't expect to see you in town, Mr. Lane," Shannon said. He knew that Lane's injuries made travel so difficult for him that he seldom came in to Dry Wells.

"I didn't want to bring him," his daughter said, "but he insisted."

"Come on inside, Mr. Lane," Shannon said. "You must be tired."

"Martha," Lane said to his daughter, "why don't you take the wagon and go visit one of your lady friends? I'll stay here and talk with Clay until you come back for me."

When she had driven away, Lane laboriously climbed onto the boardwalk and eased himself into one of the chairs that sat beside the office door.

"I suppose you've heard about me killing Pete Catlett," Clay Shannon said.

"Half the territory's heard about you killing Pete Catlett," Lane replied. "You were lucky to get out of it with nothing but a bruised shoulder."

"I see you've been talking to Doc Carson," Shannon said.

"Everybody around town is talking to everybody else about it," Lane said. "You've stirred up a hornet's nest, son."

Shannon told him about the message he had just received from Catlett's gunman.

"Tomorrow morning, eh?" Lane said. "I figured once Old Man Catlett heard the news about you shooting his son, it wouldn't take him long to get here. He isn't the forgiving type."

"So I've heard," Shannon said gloomily.

"Will any of the townspeople help you?"

"Doc Carson might. The rest will probably all be hiding in their root cellars when the Catletts arrive."

"Carson's a good man, but he's a doctor, not a gunfighter. At a time like this, the last thing a lawman needs is to have an amateur getting in the way."

"I'll keep him out of it," Shannon said. "Besides, when the shooting is all over, I may need his services."

"So, how are you going to handle it?"

"I don't know," Shannon replied. "I guess that will depend on when they come and how they come."

They sat in silence for awhile, each with his own thoughts. At length Lane roused himself.

"Have you been practicing with that six-gun like I told you?" he asked.

"Yes," Shannon said. "There hasn't been a lot of time, but I've done as much as I could."

"Good," Lane said, getting painfully to his feet. "Then let's go out back and see if it's helped any. Maybe I can give you some more useless advice."

They went out behind the office to a spot where only the empty prairie lay beyond. Lane had Shannon draw and fire at some tin cans and whiskey bottles placed on a row of fence posts. Twenty minutes later they were back again on the boardwalk in front of the office. Shannon sat down in one of the chairs and began cleaning and reloading the six-gun. Tom Lane lowered himself carefully into the other chair.

"You're even faster than you were the other day," Lane said approvingly, "and your accuracy is amazing. The practice has helped, no doubt about it. But let me give you one last piece of advice, Clay. Shooting at bottles and cans isn't the same as shooting at a man."

"My father often said that, too," Shannon said. "But I have shot at a man, Mr. Lane. I killed Pete Catlett, remember. I wish I hadn't, but I did."

"You fired then in anger and excitement, with your pistol already drawn and at point-blank range. It's a lot different to stand up in cold blood ten yards away from an armed man and draw against him, knowing it's kill or be killed."

Shannon finished loading the pistol and dropped it back into his holster.

"I know you're right and I know you want to help me, Mr. Lane," he said, "but there's no use trying to discourage me. I have to do this."

Lane uttered a sigh of resignation.

"I know you do, son," he said. "I just want you to understand what you'll be up against."

"I understand that all too well," said Shannon somberly.

Lane's daughter drove up in the wagon.

"Let's get on home, Dad," she said. "You've done enough for one day."

Lane climbed onto the seat beside her.

"I haven't done nearly enough, Martha," he told her. "Clay needs help, and nobody's helping him."

"I'm sure Clay will be fine," she said huffily. "I don't want you getting mixed up in this, Dad. You aren't a lawman anymore." She flashed a look of irritation at Shannon, and drove off. Once, before they were out of sight, Lane turned and waved to Shannon. Shannon waved back, and then they were gone.

As darkness fell, Shannon came out of the restaurant and walked slowly back to the office. Again he had not been very hungry, but he had forced himself to eat something just as a matter of principle. Once in the office, he sat at the desk for a time, fidgeting. Finally he took a repeating rifle out of the gun rack and went out the door, locking it behind him. He began a slow tour of the town, the nightly check his father had always made to be sure all was quiet. He tested each door he passed to see that it was locked, then went through the alleyways between the buildings to conduct a similar inspection of the rear doors as well.

Back on the main street again, Shannon noted with amusement that there was almost no one outside that evening. Only the saloon seemed to be showing any sign of life. Approaching the barroom doors, he could hear the laughter and music within. As he passed by on the boardwalk, he overheard someone inside, seated near the door, talking loudly.

"They'll get him sure," a deep voice was saying in an alcoholic slur.

"Aw, come on," a second voice said, "he's a good kid. He might take 'em."

"Don't make me laugh," a third voice said. "He hasn't got a chance, and you know it. He'll be dead ten minutes after they ride in."

"Bet you five bucks they smoke him before he even clears leather," the deep voice said.

"No bet," the third voice said. "He's as good as dead. Here, let's have another drink."

Shannon hesitated, debating whether or not he should go inside and confront the speakers. Then he thought better of it, and continued on into the night. Telling the truth, he decided, was not a crime, however depressing the truth might be.

Distracted by his thoughts, he failed to notice that he was passing the mouth of a particularly dark alley. Before he could react, two men had leaped out of the shadows and pinned his arms to his sides. Both men reeked of whiskey, but they held him firmly in their grasp.

A third man ran up, seized Shannon's rifle, and jerked it away from him.

"Take it easy, kid," the third man said. "Just hold still and you won't get hurt."

"Get his six-gun," one of the men holding Shannon's arms said. Shannon felt the revolver being pulled from his holster.

Shannon cursed his own carelessness. Had the Catletts arrived early and ambushed him? He was a fool to have let these men jump him. It was a mistake no experienced lawman would have made, and it might prove to be a fatal one.

"What's this all about?" he asked, playing for time.

"We want you out of town, Shannon," one of his captors replied. "Tonight."

"Yeah," one of the others said. "The folks in this town don't like the idea of what might happen to them if you make the Catletts any madder than they already are. So just get on your horse and hit the trail. Then you're safe, we're safe, the town's safe, and everybody's happy."

"Whaddaya say, kid?" the man on his right asked. "We're askin' you nicely. Will you go?"

"Not likely," Shannon replied.

The third man stepped forward and Shannon could see a knife blade gleaming in the lamplight from a nearby window.

"Listen to me, Shannon," the man said, waving the knife in front of Shannon's face. "You're goin', or you're gonna be found in that alley tomorrow with your throat cut. Either way, Old Man Catlett will be satisfied. So, it's up to you. Well?"

Shannon thought quickly. He knew he could not break the grip on his arms before the knife-wielder had plunged the blade into him.

"You win," he said. "I didn't want to hang around here anyhow. No need to get rough about it."

"That's more like it," the man with the knife said, lowering the blade. "Where's your horse?"

"In the corral at the house," Shannon replied.

"Okay," the man holding his right arm said. "We'll just walk along with you to make sure you don't change your mind."

He released his grip, freeing Shannon's arm. Shannon immediately twisted away from the other man and pulled out the second revolver he had stuck into his belt before he left the office.

"Look out!" one of the men yelled. "He's got another gun!"

"Surprise, surprise," Shannon said. The man with the knife leaped at him, and Shannon whipped the barrel of the revolver hard across his temple. The man went down without a sound as the knife skittered away in the dirt. Shannon whirled and slapped the six-gun across the face of the second man, who also fell heavily to the earth. Then Shannon shoved the gun's muzzle up against the abdomen of the last of the three men, a fat man who had frozen in disbelief when Shannon had pulled the second revolver.

"If you move," Shannon said, "I'll blow you into next week. Now drop the gunbelt."

"Okay, t-take it easy," the man stammered. "This wasn't my idea anyway."

"Sure it wasn't," Shannon said. "Now, you grab your two playmates by the collar and drag them over to the jail, and no tricks. I'll be right behind you, and I'll kill you if you so much as stumble on the way. *Move!*"

He retrieved his rifle and the first six-gun from the

dirt where they had been thrown, and then followed with the second revolver cocked as the fat man hauled his limp confederates across the street toward the jail. The dead weight of the two unconscious men was a heavy load, and the fat man panted and wheezed as he pulled. Each time he exhaled, alcoholic fumes filled the night. When they reached the office, Shannon locked him in a cell and then dragged the other two, still unconscious, across the floor into the jail and locked them in also. Then he went back into the office and sat down at the desk, still a little unsteady after the unexpected encounter.

The door opened and old Ben came in, his eyes alight.

"I saw you comin' across the street with them three," Ben said. "You want me to stick around tonight?"

"No thanks, Ben," Shannon said. "Just keep an eye on things for a few minutes while I finish my rounds, will you?"

He resumed his tour of the town where he had left off, but this time he was fully alert and each alleyway and dark shadow was carefully inspected before he passed it. *Doc's right,* Shannon thought. *I'm learning. I just hope I learn soon enough.*

There was a light on in the doctor's office, and as Shannon neared the door Doc Carson came out, stretching and yawning.

"Evening, Clay," he said. "Everything all right?"

"Quiet as a tomb," Shannon said, instantly regretting the comparison. "Look, Doc, I want you to stay out of it tomorrow. Don't try to help me. I'll do what's necessary. Agreed?"

The doctor hesitated, frowning in discontent.

"All right, Clay, whatever you want," he said finally. "It's your play. But it's getting late now. You'd better go home and get some rest."

"I'll rest tomorrow night," Shannon said. "One way or the other."

He finished his rounds and went back to the office. He sent Ben home, then checked the jail. His three assailants were snoring peacefully in their cells. Shannon closed the door between the office and the jail, lay down on the bunk in the office, and tried to go to sleep. Finally, about one o'clock, he dozed off, but it was not a restful slumber. Nightmarish images of what had been, and what might soon be, tormented him throughout the long night.

Chapter Seven

The morning was hot, and there was a slight haze in the air that gave promise of an even hotter afternoon. The sultry breeze was kicking up dust devils along the street as Shannon stepped out of the office. Old Ben arrived with breakfast for the three prisoners.

"After you've fed them, turn them loose," Shannon said.

"But they tried to kill you, son," Ben said in astonishment.

"Not really," Shannon said. "They tried to run me out of town, that's all. Besides, they were drunk. I doubt if they'll even remember what they did. We'll keep their guns, but you can let them go."

Shannon hurried back to his house to tend to the horses. As he saddled the buckskin, he saw with disgust that one of the stallion's shoes was loose. He walked the horse back to the marshal's office, tied it at the hitchrail, and went inside.

"Watch the place for a while, will you Ben?" he asked. "I have to go up to the blacksmith's. My horse has a loose shoe. I'm sorry to leave you here alone again, but if I'm chasing the Catletts today or they're chasing me, I don't want a lame horse under me. I'll be as quick as I can. Lock the door and don't open it for anybody until I get back."

The blacksmith's shop was at the far end of the main street, near the edge of town. Shannon watched impatiently as the smith replaced the buckskin's shoe.

"Think there'll be some fireworks today, Clay?" the blacksmith asked.

"Maybe," Shannon said. "We'll see."

The blacksmith heard the tightness in Shannon's voice and looked sharply at him.

"You scared, kid?" he asked sympathetically.

"No," Shannon lied.

The shoeing went slowly, and Shannon became restless.

"Hurry it up, will you Sam?" he asked. "I have to get back to the office."

"Be through in a minute," the blacksmith said. "Can't rush a good job, you know."

A gunshot sounded from somewhere up the street, quickly followed by another. Shannon cursed. The blacksmith had not yet finished, so Shannon left the horse there and started running toward the source of the gunfire, his revolver in hand. It was several hundred yards back to the center of town, and by the time he reached it he was perspiring and out of breath. In the street ahead of him, a small crowd had gathered around a figure lying in the dust. Shannon pushed his way through.

"What is it?" he asked. "What's happened?"

"It's old Tom Lane," someone said.

Shannon knelt beside Lane. Blood was trickling down the old man's left arm and oozing from a bullet hole in his thigh. He raised his head and looked up at Shannon.

"I'm sorry, Clay," he said with a gasp. "The Catletts were headed for your office. I tried to stop them."

"The Catletts are here?" Shannon asked.

"Yeah. I figured they'd be coming in about now, so I waited for them. I thought I might be able to cut down the odds for you a little, but they got me before I could even knock one of them off his horse. I'm sorry, boy."

"Where are they now, Mr. Lane? I don't see them in the street."

"I don't know, son. I didn't see much after they plugged me."

Lane fell back, breathing rapidly and gritting his teeth against the pain of his wounds.

"I saw them, Clay," someone said. It was Mitch Harris, the owner of the hotel. "After they shot poor Tom they went into the saloon," Harris said. "Probably getting likkered up before they come for you. Guess they needed some liquid courage before they faced anybody but one old man."

Clay got to his feet and looked around.

"You and you," he said, pointing at two of the onlookers. "Get Mr. Lane over to Doc Carson's. Hurry! The rest of you . . . just exactly what happened here?"

Etta McCall, the woman who ran the restaurant, stepped forward.

"It was that Catlett trash, all right," she said, her voice quavering. "They rode into town just a few minutes ago. Old Tom was waiting for them on the boardwalk in front of my restaurant. When he saw them coming he got up and hobbled right out into the middle of the street, cane and all. He held up his hand to stop them, and then told them to turn around and get out of town. They just laughed at him. Then one of them drew on him and fired. Tom went down before he could shoot back."

Lane's daughter, Martha, came running up.

"What is it?" she cried. "Where's my father?"

"They're taking him over to the doctor's office," Shannon said. "I thought you and he went back out to the ranch last evening, Martha. What was he doing here in town?"

"He insisted we hitch up the wagon and drive in again this morning," she said. "I tried to talk him out of it, but he said he had an appointment to keep. He wouldn't tell me anything more. Why did he come, Clay?"

"He was trying to save my life. He knew the Catletts would be here this morning, and he decided to try to stop them from killing me."

"Oh, the old fool!" she exclaimed. "He still thinks he's a lawman."

"He may be old and he may be a fool for what he did today," Shannon said, "but he's still a lawman, Martha. In his mind he's still carrying the star, and he did what any good lawman would do. He tried to stop trouble from coming to his town. You should be proud of him. I certainly am. Now go on over to the doctor's and see how badly he's hurt."

He turned to the crowd. Ed Miles was there.

"Did you see this, Ed?" Shannon asked.

"Yeah," Miles said. "I wish I hadn't."

"How many of them are there?"

"Six, I think. The old man, Pete's brothers Frank and Al, and two or three guys I never saw before. Probably some of the Catletts' hired guns."

"Which one shot Tom Lane?"

"It was the older brother, Frank. Knocked Tom down with the first shot, then rode over and put another bullet in him while he was lying on the ground."

"And then they went into the saloon?"

"That's right," Miles said. "Look, their horses are still tied out front."

Shannon looked, squinting against the morning glare as he tried to see the front of the saloon. There were six horses standing at the saloon's hitchrail.

"All right," Shannon said. "Thanks, Ed. Now, all of you, get off the street. Stay indoors until this is settled. I don't want anybody else to get shot."

The crowd speedily started to melt away.

"Good luck, Marshal," someone called.

"Thanks," Shannon said. "I'm going to need it."

As he approached the saloon, he saw that a man was sitting on the boardwalk in front of it, his chair tilted back against the wall. As Shannon drew near, the man abruptly jumped up and hastened into the saloon. *A lookout,* Shannon told himself. *The rest of them will be coming out now. All six of them. Think fast, Shannon.*

He tried to recall the things Tom Lane had told him the day they had talked at the Lane ranch. What was it the old marshal had said? *"Whenever possible, fight with the sun at your back, because then it will be in your opponents' eyes."* And he had said something else, too, something very important. *"If the circumstances permit it, try to come up behind them. The element of surprise is often your best weapon."*

Shannon glanced up at the sun. *If I can get around to the other side of the saloon,* he thought, *I'll be behind them when they come out, and they'll be facing the sun when they turn around. They let me outflank them once, so maybe they'll be dumb enough to let me do it again.*

He left the main street and ran down the narrow passageway that led to the rear of the saloon. Still moving rapidly, he crossed in back of the saloon and came up the other side. As he neared the front of the building again, he pressed his shoulders against the wall and waited, six-gun in hand. There was a sudden stirring inside the saloon, and the swinging doors squeaked loudly several times. Boots sounded on the boardwalk and Shannon could hear someone rushing out into the street.

Peering around the front corner of the saloon, he saw that six men were now strung out across the main street. They were all facing away from him, looking down toward the marshal's office. Old Man Catlett stood in the center of the line, holding a bullwhip. On his right was the oldest brother, Frank, while the youngest brother, Al, stood at the old man's left. Two of the remaining men were unknown to Shannon, but the sixth man was the swarthy gunman who had delivered Catlett's message the previous afternoon. All of the six were dirty and unshaven, and one of them was leisurely scratching his armpit as he waited.

What a zoo, Shannon thought. *Six unwashed gorillas who want to kill me in a town that literally doesn't care whether I live or die. Well, I volunteered for this, so I guess I can't complain. Like the saying goes, I shouldn't have signed up if I couldn't take a joke.*

He cocked the revolver's hammer, then strode deliberately out into the street, a few yards to the rear of the six men. The morning sun was behind him now, and the killers would be looking directly into it when they turned around to face him.

"Looking for someone, gentlemen?" he asked.

The six whirled around, startled.

"It's Shannon," Frank Catlett said, shading his eyes against the sun. "Well, well, well."

Old Man Catlett stepped forward a pace.

"You killed my boy, Shannon," he said. "Now I'm gonna make you pay for it, in spades." He uncoiled the bullwhip, his eyes gleaming in anticipation.

"Pete was trying to kill me, Mr. Catlett," Shannon said. "I acted in self-defense. I'm sorry about the whole thing, but that's the way it was. Now I'm asking you to put down your weapons before someone else gets hurt."

"You're the one who's going to get hurt, Shannon," Old Man Catlett said. "Cover him, boys."

"I'll gut-shoot the first man who touches his holster," Shannon barked, raising the cocked revolver. The Catlett men hesitated, seeing that Shannon had the drop on them.

"He can't get us all," Frank Catlett said with a sneer. "Plug him!"

"I'll tell you just once more," Shannon said. "The first man who draws, dies. Mr. Catlett, please listen to me. None of this is necessary. I don't want to kill you or anybody else. Don't make me do it."

For a moment longer, the Catlett men continued to hesitate. Shannon stood there alone, in the middle of the street, waiting, his life hanging in the balance. He knew that if they drew on him, he could never get all six before they gunned him down. *Frank will draw first,* he told himself. *Then the old man, then the rest. I'll get Frank and the old man, but the rest will get me. Well, perhaps they'll back down instead. Perhaps.*

Frank Catlett cursed and went for his gun.

After that it was all a blur. Shannon shot Frank in the heart, then fired at Old Man Catlett. The old man threw up his arms and went over on his back, his bullwhip flying through the air. But even as Shannon cocked his six-gun for the third shot, he saw that, as he had anticipated, he was going to be too late. The others had their guns out, bringing them up, their thumbs pulling back the hammers. Shannon fired once more, knocking Al Catlett off his feet. Then there was no more time. He found himself looking down three gun muzzles, waiting for them to belch flame and end his life.

At that moment the street exploded in gunfire. Rifles were cracking from doorways, and Shannon heard the hollow boom of a shotgun. All three of the remaining gunmen crumpled to the ground, their weapons still unfired. Two of them lay unmoving where they fell, but one was still alive. He struggled to get up again, reaching for his fallen six-gun as he tried to regain his feet. Another shotgun bellowed, and the man collapsed once more.

Shannon stood there for a moment, bewildered, gazing with astonishment at the six downed men. Then he looked up at the buildings from which the rifle and shotgun fire had come. Fifty feet away, Tom Lane was braced against a doorframe, awkwardly levering another cartridge into the chamber of his rifle with his unwounded arm. Then Doc Carson stepped into view, holding a double-barreled shotgun. Someone else was coming out of the general store, and Shannon saw that it was Ed Miles, the storekeeper, with a smoking rifle in his hand. Next old Ben walked out of the marshal's office, shoving two fresh cartridges into the shotgun he was carrying. He began checking the men lying in the street to see if they were all dead.

Shannon stared at his four rescuers, speechless, as they moved toward him.

"You all right, Clay?" asked the doctor, swinging the shotgun back over his shoulder.

"I think so," Shannon said, dazed by the sudden ferocity of it all.

Tom Lane came hobbling forward. His leg and shoulder were bandaged and he winced in pain with each step.

"Sure, he's all right," Lane said. "Good shooting,

son. You got the old man and Frank and Al too before they could even clear leather."

"Yeah," Ed Miles said, grinning broadly. "Not one of those rattlesnakes got off a single shot."

Shannon uncocked his six-gun and holstered it. His knees were shaking, and he had to resist a strong desire to sit down in the middle of the street.

"W-What . . . ," he stammered. "Why did you . . ."

"I told the mayor the other evening to form a vigilance committee," Miles said, still grinning. "He wouldn't do it, so the four of us formed our own."

Shannon looked again at the corpses sprawled in the dust.

"Lucky for me you did," he said, trying to keep his voice steady. His hands had begun to tremble, and he hastily shoved them into his pockets to hide them from view.

"I don't know what to say," he murmured, as the full realization of what they had done sank in. "You risked your lives to help me. All of you. How can I thank you?"

"Don't try," Doc Carson said. "We're the ones who should be thanking you."

People were now pouring out into the sunlight. They gathered around the bodies, pointing and uttering exclamations of wonder. Some of them came over to shake Shannon's hand and the hands of the four who had joined the fight on his behalf. One man came up to Shannon and stood uncomfortably before him, embarrassment written on his face.

"Marshal," he said with a shamefaced grin, "I'm Bill Stover. I'm one of the ones who grabbed you last night. I'm truly sorry for what we did, Marshal. We was pretty well crocked, I guess. We wanted to scare you into leaving town, but that was all. We never meant to do you no harm." He touched the side of his skull gingerly. "Guess we got what was coming to us, didn't we?" he added.

Shannon smiled weakly. His knees were still shaking.

"I don't blame you for what you did, Bill," he said. "In your place I might have done the same."

Tom Lane was beside Shannon now, resting on his cane. His face was pale from the effects of his wounds, but he wore an expression of immense satisfaction.

"Well, Clay," he said, "I guess you're a lawman for sure now. I've never seen anything like what you just did. Congratulations, son."

"I wouldn't be here to be congratulated if it hadn't been for you and the others," Shannon said with a rueful smile. "Thank you, Mr. Lane. Thanks to all of you."

The crowd parted as if by magic and Mayor Partridge came bounding through, followed by several of the city councilmen. Partridge looked with horror at the bodies in the street and then hurried over to Shannon.

"I warned you about this, Shannon," he said shrilly. "Gunplay. Dead bodies and blood in the streets of my town. It's disgraceful. Positively disgraceful."

"Oh, shut up, Elmer," Doc Carson said. "You sound as if you'd be happier if they'd killed Shannon."

"Well," the mayor said testily, "maybe we'd have been better off if they had."

He turned to Shannon and held out his hand, palm up.

"Shannon," he said, "I want that badge. You're fired."

Shannon blinked at him, dumbfounded.

"I don't understand," he said.

"You understand all right," the mayor retorted. "I don't want any more of this kind of violence in Dry Wells. I'll find someone else to be marshal."

"You'll never find anyone who could do what Clay did today," Tom Lane said heatedly.

"Yeah," Ed Miles said. "You ought to be down on your knees thanking him, instead of asking for his badge."

"I don't care," Partridge bellowed. "He's brought us nothing but trouble, and I've had enough of it. This was a nice, peaceful town until he came along."

"It was a nice peaceful town until Pete Catlett killed Clay's father," Doc Carson shouted back. "You haven't forgotten that, have you, you ungrateful old windbag?"

"You can call me all the names you want," Partridge said haughtily, "but Shannon's through as marshal. The badge, Shannon. Give it to me."

Without comment, Shannon unpinned the star from his shirt and handed it to Partridge.

The mayor shoved the badge into his coat pocket and hastened off.

"Someone go find the undertaker," he brayed as he departed, "and tell him to get those bodies off my street!"

Doc Carson glared at the mayor's departing back.

"I've always disliked that man," he said. "Now I know why."

"Well, son," Lane said, "I guess you've just learned something else about being a lawman. Rule Five is, don't expect any thanks from the people you protect. I've seen it in a dozen towns. When they need you, they love you. When the shooting's over, they can't get rid of you fast enough."

The four of them accompanied Shannon to the marshal's office, where Shannon collected the few personal belongings his father had left there.

"What are you going to do now, Clay?" Doc Carson asked.

"I'll give him a job in the store," Ed Miles said. "Good pay and regular hours, Clay. What about it?"

"No thanks, Ed," Shannon replied. "I appreciate it, but I think I'll move on. There must be some other town in the territory that needs a lawman."

"You still want to be a lawman, after what happened here?" Doc Carson asked incredulously.

Tom Lane laughed.

"I warned you, Clay," he said. "It gets into your blood. If you keep carrying a star, pretty soon it's too late to quit, because you can't imagine yourself doing anything else. Think it over, boy. Is that the life you really want for yourself?"

"It was good enough for my father, and it was good enough for you, Mr. Lane," Shannon said. "I think I'll give it a try."

Lane's daughter bustled in and grasped her father's arm.

"Come on, Dad," she said. "You've lost a lot of blood and you need to lie down."

Lane shook off her grip.

"You're absolutely sure about wanting to be a lawman, son?" he asked.

"Yes," Shannon said, his jaw set firmly. "Absolutely."

"Tell you what," Lane said. "I know the city marshal over in Longhorn. I'll write to him, asking him to give you a job. If you must be a lawman, he's a good man to work for. It's a tough town, though. A cattle town. One of the worst. You'll earn your pay."

"That's fine with me, Mr. Lane," Shannon said. "Thanks."

"When do you think you'll be leaving?" Lane asked.

"I'll have to sell the horses first," Shannon replied. "All but the buckskin. I expect Hank Stone down at the livery stable will buy them. He's already made me an offer on them. I'll see him this afternoon, and if he takes them, I'll be on my way in the morning."

"I'll write the letter tonight," Lane said, "and send it off to Longhorn tomorrow. I'll give you a copy of it to take along with you, just in case. You can pick it up on your way out of town."

Chapter Eight

It was another hot morning in Dry Wells. Clay Shannon put his foot into the stirrup and mounted his horse. As he settled himself in the saddle, he looked back at the house that had been his home and the corral that had held the horses he loved. The corral was empty now, and so was the house.

"Well, my friend," Shannon said to the buckskin, "I guess it's just you and me now."

He turned the horse and rode up the main street of Dry Wells for the last time.

He stopped first at the marshal's office to say goodbye to old Ben. The jailer was sitting at the desk, humming a tune, when Shannon came in. A badge now adorned Ben's ragged shirt.

"I see you've got a new job," Shannon said with a chuckle.

"Sure enough, son," Ben said. "The mayor made me the town marshal. What do you think of that?"

71

"I'm sure you'll make a fine marshal, Ben," Shannon said. "Just don't get any blood on Mayor Partridge's streets."

He stopped next at Doc Carson's office.

"So long, Doc," he said, shaking the doctor's hand. "Thanks again for all you've done."

"So long, Clay," the doctor said. "It's been a privilege knowing you. May God go with you, son."

"And you, Doc. Always."

As Shannon rode away, the doctor pulled a handkerchief out of his pocket and furtively wiped his eyes.

Shannon dismounted in front of Tom Lane's ranch house and knocked on the door. Tom Lane was waiting for him in the easy chair by the sitting room window. Lane handed him a letter, neatly folded.

"Well, son," he said, "this ought to get you a deputy marshal's badge in Longhorn, if you still want it."

"I want it, Mr. Lane. Thanks."

"Wear the star with pride, Clay," Lane said in a husky voice. "Down through the years, a lot of good men have carried it with honor. Some of them, like your father, have died for it. Don't let anything tarnish it. Ever."

"I won't," Shannon said, shaking the old man's hand. "That's a promise. Good-bye, Mr. Lane, and thank you again. Thanks for everything."

Shannon placed the letter carefully in his shirt as he left the house. Then he remounted the buckskin, picked up the reins, and set out along the dusty road to meet his destiny.

Chapter Nine

Shannon rode the buckskin slowly along the main street of Longhorn, Kansas, marveling at what he saw. Clearly, the city's reputation as a boom town was well-deserved.

After the end of the Civil War, Texas cattlemen had started driving their herds north to Kansas to reach the railroad that would transport the cattle east to feed a beef-hungry nation. When the herds began to arrive, Longhorn had quickly acquired a reputation for wildness that was unequaled anywhere on the frontier. After the Texas cowhands had delivered the cattle to the stockyards, they set out to celebrate the end of their hard, dry, lonely months on the trail. They took their pay and rode into town, ready to make up for lost time in the saloons, gambling halls, and other attractions that Longhorn offered for their pleasure, and they pursued their pleasure with a fierce dedication that lasted as long as their wages did. Longhorn catered to their tastes, relieved them of their money, and then sent them south again with aching heads and empty pockets, poorer but usually no wiser. Meanwhile, Longhorn waited for the next trail herd to arrive, so that the process could begin all over again.

Thus it was that Shannon found himself riding down a wide street flanked with saloons, dance halls, poker and faro parlors, sleazy-looking hotels, and a bewildering variety of other enterprises, each crowded with men wearing big hats, chaps, and other adornments that marked them as cowpunchers. The covered board sidewalks overflowed with these Texans, all seemingly rushing headlong to get to the next place of entertainment.

However, the Texans were not the only ones who came to Longhorn. Here and there a group of buffalo hunters could be seen, holding the heavy rifles that were the tools of their cruel trade. Trappers wearing their fringed leather jackets moved among the crowds. Gamblers, dance hall girls, freighters, and an occasional soldier joined in the mix that flowed along the boardwalk, filling it with noise and color. The noise was a mixture of the sound of tinny pianos playing, the shouts of mirth and wrath ringing out of the flesh-pots that lined the walks, and, occasionally, the report of a firearm being discharged, although whether this latter was in joy or anger, Shannon could not tell.

Even the center of the street was crowded with people hurrying in various directions, and wagons and buggies of all descriptions moved up and down the thoroughfare. The buckskin shied as a rumbling freight wagon veered dangerously close, and Shannon stroked the nervous animal's neck to soothe him.

"Amazing, isn't it?" he said to the buckskin as he looked around at the chaos. "Dry Wells was never like this."

Ahead of Shannon, the traffic ebbed and flowed around two men who were engaged in a fistfight in the middle of the street. The flying fists were supplemented with bites, kicks, and ferocious yells from the combatants. Shannon eased the buckskin over toward the side of the street to avoid them as he passed.

He had gone only a few yards beyond the brawling cowboys when gunshots sounded up ahead. Shannon could see that two more Texans were standing in the street with whiskey bottles in their fists, whooping joyously and firing their revolvers into the air. Shannon started to go around them, but as he was about to pass safely by, a young man dressed in a white shirt and black string tie stepped off the boardwalk and advanced toward the celebrating cowhands. Shannon saw that there was a deputy city marshal's badge pinned to the young man's shirt pocket. Smiling affably, the deputy ambled unhesitatingly up to the two cowmen. All three of them were directly in Shannon's path, and he reined up, unable for the moment to get by.

"Okay, boys," the deputy said. "Fun's over. Let's have those guns."

Before the Texans could respond, another trail herder leaped off the boardwalk and rammed a six-gun's muzzle into the deputy's back.

"Eeee-hah!" he shouted. "Looky here, boys, I've

caught me a genuine Kansas lawman. Don't move, law dog, or I'll blow a hole in you so wide a Texas steer could run through it."

"Hey," one of the other two said, "is he the same tin star who cracked Cad Bennet's skull last night and hauled him off to jail? I hear old Cad ain't woke up yet."

"Naw, it's not the same one," the second cowhand said, "but one star-packer's like another. They're all in it together. What'll we do with him? Shoot him or just bust his head like they did Cad's?"

The man with the gun shoved into the lawman's back thumbed back the hammer of his weapon.

"Let's shoot him," he said. There was a vicious light in his eyes, and Shannon saw that the man actually intended to carry out the threat. Quickly Shannon kicked the buckskin forward. He pulled his rifle out of its saddle scabbard and swung the barrel of the weapon down hard on the gunman's wrist. The man uttered a squeal of pain and fell to his knees, dropping the revolver into the dust as he gripped his injured arm.

"Take it easy there, cowboy," Shannon said. "That's the law you're talking to."

The deputy had his own revolver out now, and had stepped back so he could cover all three men.

"Shuck those gunbelts, you two," he said, retrieving the third man's revolver from the street where it had fallen. "Now both of you get on out of here before I run you in. You can pick up your guns at the city marshal's office on your way out of town."

"What about Clancy?" one of them asked, indicating the third man, who was still on his knees, groaning.

"He's going to jail. Now get moving unless you want to join him."

The two Texans sullenly moved away.

The deputy clamped a pair of handcuffs onto the fallen cowhand's wrists. The man grunted in pain as the steel tightened on his damaged arm. Shannon was still sitting on the buckskin, watching all of this with fascination. The deputy looked up at him with a grateful smile.

"Thanks, friend," he said. "I reckon you just saved my bacon. I'm Steve Warren. May I ask your name?"

"It's Shannon, Clay Shannon. Glad to meet you."

"Oh, so you're Shannon? Marshal Hollister mentioned you. Said you were coming to town to join up with us."

"I'd like to," Shannon said, "if the Marshal will take me on."

Warren laughed.

"He'll take you on, all right," he said. "We're short-handed as it is, and another deputy will be mighty welcome. You on your way to see Hollister now?"

"Yes," Shannon said. "I thought I'd better check in with him first."

"Fine," Warren said. "If you want to tag along while I run this Texas terror in, I'll show you the way. These days a stranger can get lost in Longhorn mighty fast."

Shannon dismounted and, holding the buckskin's reins, trailed after Warren as the deputy weaved his way through the crowd, propelling the handcuffed cowboy in front of him. When they reached the City

Marshal's office, Warren escorted his prisoner up onto the boardwalk.

"Come on in, Shannon," Warren said. "This is home."

Shannon tied his horse to the hitchrail and followed him inside.

The office was large, huge to Shannon's eyes compared to the little cubbyhole that had been his father's office in Dry Wells. He found himself standing in a broad room with several desks in it. Beyond the desks, an open door led into what was obviously the jail. A long row of cells could be seen through the doorway, all of them occupied.

"Hang on while I get our friend here locked up," Warren said, "and then I'll take you in and introduce you to Marshal Hollister."

Warren moved across the office, still pushing the Texas miscreant before him.

"Hey, Zeke," he shouted. "Got a customer for you."

A small man holding a ring of keys came out of the jail, looking unhappy.

"Not another one," he said. "Place is jammed now. What's the charge?"

"Let's try assault on a police officer, obstruction of justice, and disturbing the peace," Warren said. "When he goes before the judge tomorrow, the fine for all those offenses should come to about a hundred dollars, and maybe that will put enough of a dent into his bankroll to keep him out of trouble until he goes south again. Be right back, Shannon."

He returned from the cells shortly, folding his handcuffs and putting them out of sight under his coat.

"Come on," he said. He went to a closed door at one side of the large office and knocked loudly.

"Somebody to see you, Bob," he called.

Marshal Robert Hollister was a big man with broad shoulders and a friendly smile. When Warren introduced them, Hollister pumped Shannon's hand enthusiastically and waved him to a chair.

"Glad to meet you, Clay," Hollister said. "Tom Lane wrote to me about you. He says you're a good lawman, and a compliment like that from Tom Lane is high praise indeed. I can use you, if you want the job. How about it?"

"There's nothing I'd like more," Shannon said happily. "Thanks, Marshal. When do I start?"

"The sooner the better. But first I expect you'd like to find a place to stay so you can wash off some of the trail dust and get a few hours' sleep. I'll have Steve to take you over to the Longhorn House and make sure you get a good room. Then you can have some supper and a night's rest. I'll see you here tomorrow morning. Eight o'clock all right?"

"I'll be here," Shannon said. He felt as if he had just arrived at the top of the world.

Chapter Ten

At 8:00 the following morning, Clay Shannon was sworn in as a deputy marshal of the city of Longhorn. Marshal Hollister administered the oath, then handed Shannon a shining silver badge.

"Congratulations, son," Hollister said. "This is a rough town, maybe one of the roughest in the West, and some men who put on that badge decide to take it off again after they find out what they're up against. From what Tom Lane said about you, I think you'll do just fine, but don't get careless. One mistake here can be your last."

He opened the door to the outer office.

"Now," he said, "let me introduce you to your fellow targets."

Steve Warren was sitting at a desk, filling out a report.

"Morning, Steve," Hollister said. "You've already

met Clay Shannon, our newest deputy. He's starting work today."

Warren stood up and shook Shannon's hand.

"Hello again," he said with a wry grin. "Actually, Bob," he added, turning to Hollister, "Shannon started work yesterday. While I was chatting with a couple of those Texas boys yesterday afternoon, I made a dumb mistake and let another one get behind me and put a six-gun in my ribs. If Shannon hadn't come along and discouraged him with a rifle barrel, you might be short a man this morning."

Hollister looked pained.

"Steve," he said, "you're a good deputy, but you have one fault. You're too easy-going with these Texas cowpokes. And too trusting. One of these days it's going to get you shot."

"My mother always told me to be nice to people," Warren said with a laugh.

"Your mother wasn't a deputy marshal in a trail town," Hollister replied tartly.

He turned to look at Shannon, his face grim.

"First lesson, Clay," he said. "Most of the Texans are all right, even though they tend to get a little rowdy. But some of them are real hard cases, as hard as anything Kansas ever produced. Gunslingers, wanted men, all kinds come up the trail with those herds. And even the good ones can be dangerous when they're full of whiskey, which is most of the time. Don't ever underestimate them. Keep your eyes open and your back covered, and always expect the worst. It's not a very nice way to look at things, I guess, but it's the only way to look at them if you want to stay healthy in Longhorn."

Shannon nodded. It was plain to see that his life in Longhorn was not going to be boring.

As they were talking, another deputy came into the office. He was an older man with a white mustache. His face was weathered, but there was a gleam in his eye and a spring in his step that belied his age.

"Clay Shannon," Hollister said, "meet Walt Tucker. Don't let the grey hair fool you, Clay. Walt's one of the best, and when he talks, you'll do well to listen."

"Hello, son," Tucker said, shaking hands warmly. "If there's anything I can do to help you get settled in, just let me know."

"We've got two other deputies," Hollister said. "They should be along soon. Yeah, there's Bonham now."

A tall, lean man wearing a black suit and black hat appeared in the doorway. Shannon could see that beneath his coat, the man had twin holsters tied down to his thighs. He moved with a grace that suggested to Shannon that he knew his business and would be highly proficient with the six-guns the holsters contained.

"Clay, this is Cash Bonham," Hollister said. "Cash is Longhorn's reigning fast gun. I've seen him use those two six-guns of his a couple of times, and it's impressive. Cash, this is Clay Shannon, our new deputy."

Bonham nodded at Shannon, fixing Shannon's blue eyes with his own pale green ones.

"Glad to meet you, Shannon," he said. "Welcome to the lunatic asylum."

There was a clattering of boots on the boardwalk outside the office door, and a heavyset man with a pock-marked face entered the office. He was wearing a deputy's badge and dragging behind him a much smaller man whose face was covered with blood. The heavyset deputy hauled the small man roughly across the threshold and dumped him on the floor.

"Shannon," Hollister said, "this is Bo Clagg. He believes in the firm approach, as you can see. Bo, this is our new deputy, Clay Shannon. He's here to learn from your bad example."

Bo Clagg did not make a favorable first impression. He was unshaven and there were gravy stains on his sweaty shirt. His face was puffy, and he wore an expression of ill humor that Shannon guessed was his normal state.

Clagg glanced at Shannon with bloodshot eyes, grunted a greeting, and then hauled his prisoner to his feet by the simple method of yanking on the handcuffs that bound the little man's wrists.

"Take it easy, Clagg," Hollister said. "You know I don't like to have prisoners mistreated. Why have you brought him in?"

"Aw, he was drunk," Clagg mumbled.

"Every cowhand in Longhorn is drunk," Hollister said, "and we don't usually arrest them for that. Why pick on this one? Was he causing a disturbance?"

"Naw," Clagg said, unlocking the handcuffs. "I just didn't like the way he looked at me. I don't take nothin' from these drunks."

"Put him in a cell and let him out when he sobers up," Hollister said, regarding Clagg with distaste. "Well, that's everybody, Shannon. These are the men who'll be working with you."

He turned to Walt Tucker.

"Give Shannon the grand tour, will you, Walt?" he asked. "Show him what he's gotten himself into."

Shannon walked beside Tucker as the two of them moved unhurriedly down the boardwalk. Although it was early, the walk was crowded with a colorful mixture of noisy humanity. Longhorn never slept.

"What do you think of your fellow deputies?" Tucker asked.

"Warren and Bonham seem all right," Shannon said cautiously.

"Steve Warren's a good man," Tucker said, "but like Hollister was just telling him, Steve's too easygoing for his own good."

"And Bonham?"

"Cash is a bit of a mystery. Rumor has it that he's spent as much time on the wrong side of the law as on the right side of it, and I don't doubt it. Wouldn't surprise me if there were a couple of wanted posters on him floating around somewhere. But whatever he's been in the past, he's straight as an arrow now, and if you get caught in a bad situation, he's the man you want backing you up."

"And Clagg?" Shannon said.

"Ah, yes, our resident roughneck. Be careful of him, Clay. He's one you don't want to walk into a tight spot with. For one thing, he's a bully. He likes to hit people, preferably people who can't hit back. He consistently uses force when none is needed, and he often makes a bad situation worse."

"Why doesn't Marshal Hollister get rid of him?"

"He'd like to, but at the moment he can't. Clagg's a first cousin of one of the members of the City Council, and so we have to put up with him."

"Sounds like politics is a problem here," Shannon said.

"Politics is half of this job, son. You may not like it, but you're going to have to learn to live with it, or take up some other line of work."

Tucker stopped and bent down to inspect a cowpuncher who was lying unmoving on the boardwalk. When the old deputy was satisfied that the man was merely sleeping, he continued down the walk with Shannon.

"It all comes down to simple economics," he went on. "If we were to shut down all the pleasure palaces and ran all the cowmen out of town, the people who own these dives would lose a lot of money, and they wouldn't like that a bit. So we do what we're supposed to do, which is to keep the lid on without discouraging the cattlemen from coming here. That's the way things work here, Clay, and Longhorn's no different from any other cow town when it comes to that."

As they walked, Tucker pointed out to Shannon the various establishments they passed, giving him a quick summary of the checkered history and dubious character of each.

"Is this entire town dedicated to vice?" Shannon said wonderingly.

"Oh, we had a church once," Tucker said, "but some drunken cowboys burned it down last year."

As they were passing one of the many saloons that lined the boardwalk, two men came rolling out of the door together, flailing at each other with their fists. While they were struggling, one of them reached for his belt and drew out a huge Bowie knife. Tucker stepped forward, twisted the knife out of the man's hand, and handed it to Shannon. Then he lifted the combatants up by the scruff of the neck and held them apart at arm's length.

"Okay, boys," Tucker said, "that's enough for now. If you want to fight, that's fine, but keep it friendly. No knives, no guns, no brass knuckles. Loser buys the drinks. Those are the rules. Any questions? Good. Mr. Shannon, you can give this gentleman's Arkansas toothpick back to him now."

The knife-wielder meekly returned the blade to its sheath, and the two men shuffled back into the saloon, looking chastened.

"Bet you'd have locked them up in Dry Wells, wouldn't you?" Tucker asked, grinning.

"Probably," Shannon said.

"Well, not here. This is a cattle town, and when the trail herders finish their drives and collect their wages, they're ready to howl. So the policy is that if no weapons are being used and they're not hurting anybody but themselves, we let them fight. They're going to do it anyway, and we can't lock up every man who throws a punch. Same with drunks. If they're peaceful, let 'em alone. If they're belligerent, toss them into the pokey until they sober up."

"And what's the policy if they draw a gun on you?

"Your choice. Some deputies try to buffalo the man by knocking him down with a gun barrel. I do it that way when I can, because I don't like the idea of killing some cowboy just for wanting to have fun. It usually works, if you're quick about it."

"What if it doesn't work?"

"Shoot them."

"Would the people who run the town like that?"

"Definitely not. But if you do have to kill some-body, the Marshal will back you up. Hollister's a good boss, and he knows the lawman's first commandment is to *survive*. Don't forget that, Clay, not ever. No matter what else happens, make sure that at the end of the day you go home alive."

At length Tucker ushered Shannon into one of the saloons to introduce him to the owner. It was a large place, the largest Shannon had seen in Longhorn, and it was furnished lavishly. The owner was a big man named Tank Drummond, and he greeted Shannon with a direct gaze and a firm handshake.

"Welcome to the Emerald Palace Saloon, Shannon," Drummond said. "My games are straight, my whiskey isn't watered, my girls are honest, and I don't allow any fistfights or gunplay in the saloon. If you have to make an arrest in here, my boys will back you. Walt will tell you the same thing, I'm sure."

"He's right, Clay," Tucker said. "If all the saloons in Longhorn were as well-run as the Emerald Palace, we'd have a lot less work to do."

As they were talking, a woman approached and

stood waiting expectantly to be introduced. As she waited, she eyed Shannon with undisguised interest.

"Hello, Daisy," Tucker said. There was a touch of resignation in his voice.

"Shannon," the saloon keeper said, "this is Daisy Fisher. She helps me run this place."

Daisy held out a languid hand for Shannon to take. As he awkwardly shook her hand, Shannon could not help but note that the low-cut red velvet dress she was wearing did nothing to hide the fullness of her figure.

"Pleased to meet you, ma'am," he said, hastily releasing the soft hand.

The woman smiled approvingly.

"Well, Walt," she said to Tucker, "I see this time you hired one with manners."

After a few moments more of conversation, Tucker made their excuses and steered Shannon toward the door of the saloon. As they left, Daisy Fisher waved to Shannon.

"Do come in again, Deputy," she called sweetly. "You'll always be welcome."

As they pushed out through the swinging doors, Tucker uttered a sign of relief.

"Watch out for her, son," he said. "She's been friendly with a number of deputies, sometimes a little too friendly. I guess she likes the badge, or something."

Shannon looked back over the top of the swinging doors. Daisy Fisher was still standing there, eyeing him and smiling.

*   *   *

"That restaurant down there serves pretty good food," Tucker said, pointing at a side street. "The one next to the office is a little better, but not much. Your hotel's dining room is probably the best place in town to eat, if you aren't in a hurry. They're a little short-handed there now, but the cooking is fine."

"I had breakfast at the restaurant next to the office this morning," Shannon said. "I expect I'll eat there most of the. . . ."

Muffled gunshots echoed along the street. Tucker tensed and then started running.

"Come on, Clay," he said over his shoulder. "It's time we earned our pay."

It was easy to determine the location from which the shots had come, for a crowd was gathering outside a gambling hall named The Four Jacks, rubbernecking at something through the open door. As Tucker and Shannon pushed their way inside, Steve Warren joined them. The room was long and narrow, low-ceilinged, and none too clean. Gaming tables lined the walls, and a few oil lamps tried unsuccessfully to compensate for the absence of windows. The occupants of the Four Jacks were all looking toward the rear, where a table lay overturned on the floor with cards and chips scattered around it.

As the deputies entered, a short, plump man rushed forward to meet them.

"What's all this, Denny?" Tucker said, his hand resting close to his holster.

"Deuce Ransome just shot a cowpuncher," Denny squeaked. "I think he's dead."

A man wearing a grey frock coat and ruffled white

shirt was standing with his back against the rear wall of the room. There was a smoking derringer in his hand, and he was pointing it nervously at several Texans who were crowding forward toward him. A number of other men, gamblers and townsmen by their appearance, were gathered around the man with the frock coat, glaring with hostility at the advancing cowhands. Tucker drew his six-gun and stopped several feet away from the man with the derringer. Warren came up beside him. Shannon stood behind them, trying to see what was happening.

"Everybody just stand still," Tucker said loudly. "Drop the gun, Deuce."

"It was self-defense," the gambler said. "He accused me of cheating and drew on me."

"He's lying, Marshal!" one of the cowhands yelled. "Stan never touched his gun. He just told this cardsharp to stop dealing off the bottom of the deck!"

"That ain't the way it was!" someone in the other group shouted back. "The cowboy took a shot at Deuce, and Deuce had to defend himself."

Angry protestations arose from both sides. Tucker ignored them.

"The gun, Ransome," he said again, the muzzle of the six-gun fixed unwaveringly on the frock-coated gambler. "Put it down. Now."

With a nervous glance at the Texans, Ransome laid his little pistol on the floor in front of him.

"Now kick it over here," Tucker said.

"Come on, boys, let's get the tinhorn!" one of the Texas faction shouted. "String him up from a lamp post!"

They started to move forward again.

"Now *hold it*!" Tucker bellowed. "That man's under arrest. Let the law deal with him." The Texans hesitated for an instant, then lunged toward the unfortunate gambler. Ransome's supporters uttered a barrage of expletives and leaped into the fray, fists swinging.

Tucker sighed.

"Come on," he said to Warren and Shannon. "No rest for the weary."

Tucker and Warren charged forward and started grabbing people and throwing them aside. Shannon quickly followed and began doing the same, as the three deputies waded through the combatants toward the besieged gambler. Almost instantly, those who had been shoved aside scrambled up and launched an attack on the struggling lawmen. Shannon found himself caught in a bear hug from behind. He drove an elbow into the man's ribs and ripped the grasping hands from around his chest. Turning, he delivered a straight right to his assailant's chin, and the man went down in a heap on the dirty floor.

Someone had jumped on Warren's back, and Shannon took hold of the attacker's collar and pulled him away. Tucker was caught between two cowhands, both intent on driving their fists into his face. Shannon drew his six-gun and brought it down on the head of one, then slammed it into the jaw of the other. A chair flew through the air and struck Shannon in the back. He turned and delivered another blow of the gun barrel as the thrower of the chair launched himself forward.

By now Tucker was down with several men on top of him, pummeling him. Warren was trying to fend off another man wielding a chair, and Shannon stumbled forward to aid him. Before he could intervene, however, a lowered shoulder crashed into him from the left side and he found himself on the floor under at least four men who were all punching and kicking him.

Shannon felt a moment of panic. With the odds some ten or twelve to one, the three deputies were losing the battle. Shannon heard Warren yelp in pain. Tucker was roaring angrily, but the roars were muffled by the bodies now lying on top of him. Shannon dodged a swinging boot and tried to roll away from the men who were clutching and striking at him, but there were too many of them, and he couldn't free himself. In desperation, he drove the gun barrel into the stomach of one of them, then whipped an elbow up under the chin of another. Both men collapsed on the floor. Shannon was just regaining his feet when two more men jumped him from behind. He felt the six-gun being pried from his hand, and real fear gripped him. If they got his gun . . .

The blast of a .45 caliber revolver shook the walls of the narrow room. Squawks of dismay arose, and everyone turned to see who was firing. Cash Bonham was standing there with both guns drawn and cold menace on his face. The fighting stopped abruptly, and a sudden silence descended on the room.

"That's enough!" Bonham said. "You people get away from those deputies, and then stand still. I'll kill the first man who touches a gun."

The men who had been attacking Shannon scrambled to their feet and backed away. Steve Warren wriggled out of the pile of men who had been on top of him and began to push them one by one over against the nearest wall. Walt Tucker was tossing bodies aside like cordwood, trying to get at the unfortunate Deuce Ransom, who was lying on the floor with blood streaming down his cheek.

"He's alive," Tucker said. The deputy's grey hair was disheveled and he was breathing heavily. Steve Warren was holding a handkerchief to his bloody nose and bending over the victim of the shooting.

"So's this one," he said. "His skull's only creased. You people were about to hang a man for no reason."

Shannon got painfully to his feet, still gasping for breath. His shirt was torn, his ribs ached, and he had a bruise on his left cheek where someone had connected with a roundhouse right.

Walt Tucker limped over to him. There was blood in the corner of his mouth and a large swelling over his right eye.

"You still in one piece, Clay?" he asked anxiously.

"I think so," Shannon replied.

Tucker chuckled.

"Well, son," he said, "welcome to Longhorn."

Chapter Eleven

The next morning at five minutes before 7:00, Shannon came down the stairs from his room to the lobby of the hotel. A pretty, dark-haired girl was behind the desk, writing something. Shannon had noticed her working there before, but had not yet spoken to her. As he limped past the desk, she looked up.

"Are you all right, Mr. Shannon?" she asked.

"I'm fine," Shannon said. "Just a few aches and pains. I'm sorry, I don't know your name."

"It's Marian, Marian Thomas. You look tired. Can I get you anything?"

"Well, I wouldn't mind a cup of coffee if you have some handy."

The girl went into the dining room and returned with a steaming cup.

"I hear there was another killing in one of the gambling halls yesterday," she said, handing him the cup. "That's how you got hurt, isn't it?"

"There was a shooting, but nobody was killed," Shannon said. "We had a little argument afterwards, but it wasn't much."

"It's always something here," she said. "Shootings, killings, fights every day. This is an evil place, full of evil men."

Shannon sipped the coffee. It was hot and sweet and good.

"They're not really evil," he said slowly, "not most of them, anyway. They're just human beings with ordinary human weaknesses. A town's no worse than the people in it."

"I hate it here," she said vehemently.

"Then why do you stay?"

"My father runs this hotel. He needs me. I'll leave someday, though. I'll leave as soon as I possibly can."

Shannon surveyed her over the rim of his coffee cup. *Nice-looking girl,* he thought. *She's a couple of years younger than I am, but somehow she seems older. I guess Longhorn ages people fast.*

When the cup was empty he put it down on the counter and placed a coin beside it.

"No charge," she said. "Part of the service for guests of the hotel."

"That's very nice of you," Shannon said, "but I'd rather pay. Call it 'professional ethics.' "

Reluctantly, she picked up the coin.

"Come back for supper," she suggested. "When I'm not minding the desk I work in the dining room, and I'm a pretty good cook."

Shannon thanked her and left the hotel lobby. He paused on the boardwalk to survey the street, then made his way to the nearby livery stable and saddled his horse. Walt Tucker had suggested that they go down to the stockyards that morning to meet some of the trail bosses of the cattle outfits currently in town. As Shannon walked the buckskin along the street toward the marshal's office, his thoughts returned to Marian Thomas. Something about her dark eyes and her sadness had touched him.

She certainly hates this town, he mused. *Can't say I blame her. It's certainly no place for a young girl. No wonder she's unhappy. She seems very nice, though.* He felt a sudden pang of loneliness. *Perhaps I'll get to talk to her a little more this evening,* he thought.

Walt Tucker was waiting at the office. He mounted his horse and they started toward the cattle pens at the edge of town.

"You need to get to know as many of the trail bosses as you can," he said as they rode. "Most of them come back every year, so it's just as well to get acquainted with them and their outfits. Helps you to know what to expect, and also who you need to go to if there's a problem with that particular crew. Look, there's Lon McLean, the foreman of the Box Y ranch. He's one of the best of the Texans. Let's talk with him."

McLean was a stocky man with a weather-beaten face and an air of permanent worry. Shannon reflected briefly that it must be a great responsibility, bringing a huge herd of cattle worth many thousands of dollars on such a long journey.

Tucker and Shannon dismounted, and Tucker introduced Shannon to the Box Y foreman. McLean nodded a greeting to Shannon and then looked inquiringly at Tucker.

"How's Cad Bennett doing?" he asked. "I hear your pal Bo Clagg busted Cad's head pretty good the other day."

"The doc says he'll be all right in a couple of days. Concussion, that's all."

"Most of you deputies are decent enough," McLean said, "and you usually give my boys a fair shake, but that Clagg's a real mean critter. One day he's going to go too far, and somebody's going to put a bullet in his gizzard, badge or no badge."

"We don't like him any better than you do," Tucker said, "but we're stuck with him, at least for now. Just tell your people not to get mouthy with him. It only gives him an excuse to play rough."

They talked for a few minutes about the Box Y's trip up the trail from Texas, and the going price of beef. At length Tucker and Shannon mounted up again.

"Gotta visit with some of the other outfits," Tucker said. "Is Thad Jones still here? Haven't seen his hands in town in the last day or so."

"Naw," said McLean, "they sold their cattle three or four days ago and rode out yesterday. Most of them were flat broke and all of them had hangovers."

"Not much to show for all those weeks on the trail."

"That's the life of a cowpuncher, I guess," McLean said. "See you, Walt."

They rode between the pens to another part of the

stockyard. A train was loading cattle, and a burly man with an eyepatch was supervising the process.

"That's Cliff Horrocks," Tucker said to Shannon. "He's the trail boss for the Diamond M. He's a bad one, and so is his outfit. We generally have more trouble with them than with anybody else. Those were his boys we were playing games with in the gambling hall yesterday."

As the deputies neared Horrocks, Tucker greeted him.

"Hello there, Cliff. Nice day."

"It was until you showed up," Horrocks said sourly.

Tucker introduced Shannon. Horrocks ignored the introduction.

"What about my men you beat up in the Four Jacks yesterday?" he asked Tucker. "Any of 'em hurt bad?"

"Not as bad as they hurt us," Tucker said, touching the bruise on his forehead.

"Glad to hear it. You still got 'em locked up? We need to head south pretty soon."

"About a half-dozen of them are guests of the city just now," Tucker replied. "They'll go before the judge this morning, pay their fines, and be back in the saloons within the hour."

"Wish you tin stars would take it easy on those boys," Horrocks said. "They come a long way through some bad country, and they need to make up for lost time. They don't mean no harm."

Tucker crossed one leg over his saddle and began to build a cigarette.

"Horrocks," he said, "we've got a job to do. You know that. If your people keep it reasonable, we're not going to bother them. But yesterday in that gambling hall they were about to lynch a man for a killing that never happened."

"Yeah, some Kansas tinhorn. Too bad they didn't string him up. Look, I gotta get this loading done."

"Sure, Cliff. See you before you go."

"I hope not," Horrocks said, walking away.

"Nice fellow," Shannon said. "If all his riders are as prickly as he is, it's no wonder the town has problems with the Diamond M. Is he always like that?"

"Oh, no," Tucker said. "This is one of his good days."

As they re-entered the main part of town, Tucker glanced at Shannon's holster.

"That pistol of yours is pretty old, isn't it?" he asked.

"Yes. It was my Dad's. About all he left me."

"They've got some newer models out now. I saw a mighty nice Colt in one of the gun shops a day or two ago. Want to take a look at it?"

"Not much point in it," Shannon said regretfully. "I doubt that I can afford a new six-gun just yet."

"Still, no harm in looking. What do you say?"

Shannon had already been thinking about replacing the worn revolver his father had carried for so many years. He valued it for sentimental reasons, but the weapon was outdated and the mechanism tended to hang up at times. The difference between a rough action and a smooth one might be a matter of life and death, and it was clear that in Longhorn he was going to need the best protection he could get.

"Sure, why not?" he said. "Lead the way."

The Colt Peacemaker lay in a glass showcase, resting in a satin-lined wooden box. Its dark blue steel finish glowed in the light coming through the gun shop's windows, and the smooth ivory grips were flawless. At Walt Tucker's suggestion, the gunsmith took the revolver out of the case and handed it to Shannon. Shannon opened the loading gate and inspected the cylinder to make certain it was empty, then hefted the Colt admiringly. The ivory grips slid into his hand with an ease that was astonishing, and the barrel was so well-balanced that the gun seemed to point itself effortlessly. Shannon tried the action and found it smooth as silk. The click of the hammer being pulled back and the whispering rotation of the cylinder seemed musical to Shannon. He had never seen so fine a weapon. Reluctantly, he laid it back in its lined box.

"It's beautiful," he said softly.

"Never saw one to match it," the gunsmith said with evident pride. "One in a million, I'd say. Nice holster comes with it, too." He lifted a well-oiled black gun-belt and holster from a peg behind the counter. "Look at the workmanship," he said. "Rig like that will last you a lifetime."

Shannon touched the smooth leather, then looked again at the Colt.

"How much?" he asked.

The gunsmith named the price. Shannon hesitated. It was nearly every cent he had left in the world. Still, it was an unusually nice weapon, and he did need one. The decision came quickly.

"I'll take it," he said.

Five minutes later he walked out of the gun shop with empty pockets, three boxes of .45 cartridges, and the Colt revolver that would save his life countless times in the coming years.

Chapter Twelve

That afternoon Shannon rode out of town a short distance, both to exercise the buckskin and to try out the new six-gun. He found himself delighted with it. The action was easy, the trigger was light, and the shape of the ivory grip contributed greatly to the speed of the draw. Until this time, a six-gun had seemed to Shannon to be merely a tool of the trade, a necessary part of being a lawman, but he could not help but admire the grip, balance, and ease of handling of the new weapon. Accuracy came easily with the Colt in his hand.

He left his horse at the livery stable and headed for the marshal's office, pleasantly conscious of the different feel of the new holster against his thigh.

As he passed the Emerald Palace Saloon, he heard a sudden commotion inside. He wheeled and went through the swinging doors, seeking the source of the disturbance. As he came in, two of the saloon's bouncers hurried past him holding an obviously inebriated trail herder firmly in their grip. They marched out through the swinging doors with the protesting cowboy. There was a brief scuffle, and Shannon could hear one of the bouncers warning the miscreant in no uncertain terms not to come back until he was sober and peaceful.

As Shannon started to leave again, the owner of the Emerald Palace, Tank Drummond, came over to him.

"It's okay, Marshal," he said. "Everything's under control. We try not to let trouble even get started here. Thanks for checking, though."

Daisy Fisher appeared at Shannon's elbow. She took his arm and looked invitingly up at him.

"Glad you dropped in, Deputy," she said. "Now that you're here, let's go somewhere and talk. How about my room upstairs? We'll have a nice little chat."

Shannon found himself somewhat irritated by this less than subtle offer. Although Daisy's charms were fading a little, she was still an attractive woman, but her boldness made Shannon uncomfortable.

"I can't ma'am," he said apologetically. "I'd like to, but I have to get to the office. Perhaps another time."

Daisy gave him a smile filled with promise.

"Sure, Clay. Drop back tomorrow evening. I've got a bottle of champagne I've been saving for a special occasion."

When Shannon had left the saloon, Drummond gave Daisy a quizzical look.

"He's a bit young for you, isn't he, Daisy?" he asked.

"He's old enough," Daisy Fisher replied archly.

"You might find him a little harder to get than the others," Drummond said. "For one thing, it's plain to see he doesn't like you."

"I know," Daisy said. "It'll be fun trying to change his mind."

As Shannon made his rounds that afternoon, he could not help mentally comparing Daisy Fisher with Marian Thomas, the hotel manager's daughter. The comparison did not favor Daisy. The Thomas girl was young and pretty, and she had a fresh, clean quality about her that Shannon could not define but found very attractive. The two of them often spoke politely when Marian was behind the hotel desk as Shannon passed through the hotel lobby, but since the morning when they had talked over a cup of coffee, he had not had an opportunity to have any further serious conversation with her. She was usually busy, and often her father, the hotel manager, was nearby, which effectively discouraged any but the most casual communication. However, it had not escaped Shannon's notice that when he ate in the hotel dining room, it was always Marian and not the other waitress who came to serve his food. Sometimes they exchanged a few words during the meal as she brought the food or took away the empty plates, but on these occasions there were usually people at the nearby tables, and she always carefully avoided personal subjects. She seemed to want to talk, but was hesitant to do so freely. *Well,* Shannon thought, *I suppose she'll talk to me when she's ready. No use trying to rush things.*

As he rounded a corner he saw two cowmen circling each other in the street, exchanging colorful insults. They both had knives, and they were clearly intent on using them. Shannon recognized one of the men as being a rider for the Diamond M. Shannon broke into a run toward them. The two antagonists were directly in front of one of the town's many gambling halls, and several people were standing on the walk, watching the fight eagerly. As he approached, Shannon saw with a start that Bo Clagg was one of the spectators. He was lounging against a post with a half-empty glass of beer in his hand and a sneer on his lips.

Shannon stepped between the two circling men, grasped them firmly by their shirt collars, and pulled them apart.

"What seems to be the difficulty here, boys?" he asked, holding them at arm's length from himself and each other.

"Aw," one of them said, "this Diamond M cowpoke was cheatin' me."

"What outfit do you work for?" Shannon asked.

"Box Y," the man said defiantly. "Best outfit in West Texas, and a sight better than this cheater's gang of thieves."

The Diamond M rider reddened and struggled to escape Shannon's grip.

"Calm down, cowboy," Shannon said. "If you give me any trouble you'll spend the night in jail. Now put those knives away, both of you."

When he had sent the men on their separate ways and the onlookers, disappointed, had wandered back into the interior of the gambling hall, Shannon went up to Bo Clagg, who was still leaning against the post, his beer glass now nearly empty.

"Why didn't you stop them, Clagg?" Shannon asked.

"Why should I?" Clagg replied, finishing his beer. "They was just havin' a little fun."

"Fun?" Shannon said. "They were trying to kill each other."

"So what?" Clagg said. "Good riddance, I say. I ain't riskin' my neck just to keep a couple of them idiot trail herders from cuttin' each other up."

He went back into the gambling hall and put the empty beer glass on the bar. Then, as Shannon watched through the open door, he saw the bartender hand Clagg a wad of bills. Clagg counted them, then stuffed them in his pocket and came back outside.

"Why was the bartender giving you money?" Shannon asked. "You didn't by any chance have a bet on the knife fight, did you?"

"Naw," Clagg said. "I pick up a little extra from some of these places now and then." He grinned slyly. "You know what I mean."

"Yes," Shannon said. "You mean you're taking payoffs for leaving them alone."

"Well, yeah," Clagg said, scowling. "I guess you could put it that way."

"That's extortion, Clagg."

"Ex-*what?* Aw, wise up, Shannon. A man can get rich if he's got a badge, and I ain't no dummy. Besides, everybody does it."

"Who's *everybody?*" Shannon asked hotly. "Tucker? Warren? Bonham?"

"Them? They're too dumb. They won't even take a free drink."

"Of course they won't," Shannon said. "They're better men than that. Unlike you."

Clagg glowered at him.

"I don't need any of your holier-than-thou stuff, Shannon. You better leave me alone. I'm gettin' kind of tired of you."

"The feeling is mutual," Shannon said. "Hollister ought to throw you out on your ear. You're just making things tougher for the rest of us with your strong-arm tactics and sticky fingers."

Clagg guffawed.

"Old Hollister can't fire me," he said. "Nobody can. I got friends."

Shannon forced a laugh.

"You may have political connections, Bo," he said, "but I don't think you've got a friend in the world."

Shannon returned to the office, seething. He knew full well that there were lawmen who accepted bribes or used their badges to extort money or other favors from the people they were supposed to protect. However, he had never met anyone of this sort before, and his first face-to-face encounter with corruption had upset him. The only two lawmen he had personally known were his father and Tom Lane, both of them men of the highest integrity. Now, Shannon felt demeaned by the discovery that one of his fellow deputies was crooked. Somehow, Clagg's dishonesty seemed to tarnish Shannon's own badge, and it sickened him. He realized that he was being naive, and that Clagg was not the last marshal or sheriff he would meet who was corrupt, but this did not comfort him. Both his father and Tom Lane had taught him not to dishonor his profession, not to betray the trust conferred upon him by the badge he wore. Perhaps it was because of this that Clagg's blatant immorality was so loathsome to him.

He found Marshal Hollister behind his desk in the inner office and reported to him what he had just seen. Hollister uttered an expletive, then got up and went to the nearby window. He stood there silently for a moment, looking out into the busy street.

"Clay," he said at last, "I've worked hard to find deputies who are incorruptible, people I can count on not to abuse the power that's been given to them. Tucker and Warren and Bonham are men like that, but Clagg's another story. I'm not surprised to find him collecting protection money. Everything about him is wrong for this job, and what you saw is just one more example of that."

"Are you going to fire him?" Shannon asked.

"I'd like nothing better," Hollister said, "But unfortunately, Bo's right about one thing. I can't sack him. And here comes one of the reasons."

An elderly man with mutton-chop whiskers came bustling into the office.

"Good day, Councilman Martz," Hollister said. "Meet our newest deputy, Clay Shannon."

"Yes, indeed," Martz said with a smile, pumping Shannon's hand vigorously. "I just dropped by to tell you folks what a fine job you did stopping that affair in the Four Jacks the other day. I own part of that enterprise, you know, and I certainly would hate to see its reputation besmirched by a lynching."

"I'm sure the man who was going to be lynched shares your sentiments," Hollister said dryly.

"Well, anyway," Martz said, trying to decide if Hollister was being sarcastic or not, "You boys did a good job. By the way, how is Cousin Bo getting along?"

"Not very well, Arthur," Hollister said. "I don't think he's cut out to be a lawman."

"Oh? Why do you say that?"

"He drinks too much, he consistently uses more force than he has to, and," Hollister added, glancing at Shannon, "it now appears he's a little short on professional ethics as well."

"Nonsense," Martz said. "Bo's a good boy. I expect you to give him every chance, Marshal. You need good men."

"Yes," Hollister said with a twisted smile, "I do. Unfortunately Bo's not one of them."

Martz frowned.

"Let's not have any more of that kind of talk, Bob, if you please," he said. "The City Council would be very disturbed if they thought you'd treated Bo unfairly. Well, I must be going. Nice to meet you, Mr. Stanton."

"Shannon, Mr. Martz," Shannon said. "Not Stanton."

"Well, whatever. See you later, boys."

When Martz had departed, Shannon took a deep breath, and sank into a chair.

"Incredible," he said.

"Actually, it's fairly commonplace in this business,"

Hollister replied. "Politics, influence, people putting pressure on us to do the wrong thing or not do the right thing. It's revolting, but that's the way it is. And I'll bet that when you put on that badge, you thought the only people a lawman had to fight were the outlaws."

Chapter Thirteen

Clay Shannon and Marian Thomas were walking together on a little wooded hill that overlooked the town. A grove of trees provided some shade, and a cool breeze eased the heat of the afternoon for the two young people.

Shannon had experienced a little difficulty in getting Marian to come out with him. She had refused at first, but Shannon sensed that despite her reluctance she really wanted to go, so he had persisted until she agreed.

Marian spoke sadly of the death of her mother and her loathing for Longhorn, then began to prod Shannon to talk of his earlier life.

"Surely you can't have been a lawman very long, Clay," she said. "How did it happen?"

Shannon told her a little about Dry Wells, his father's murder, and the events that followed.

"But why do you want to keep on in this job?" she asked. "You're not like the rest of them. You're intelligent, you've got an education, and I can see you don't like all the violence. How can you stand to work with a group of men who live by the gun?"

"The marshals here are mostly good men," Shannon said, thinking of Hollister, Tucker, Warren, and Bonham. "They've all got their pasts, but they're brave and honest and they do their best in an impossible situation. I could be in far worse company."

"Then what about this man Clagg?" Marian asked. "Everybody knows he's a brutal moron. He shouldn't even be a marshal."

"You're right there," Shannon said bitterly. "He fouls the badge he wears. Marshal Hollister would have fired him long ago, but Hollister's hands are tied by the dirty politics in this town."

"There's nothing that can be done?"

"I don't know," Shannon said thoughtfully. "Apparently not."

But Fate sometimes presents opportunities to those who have the courage to seize them, as Shannon was about to discover.

Shannon took Marian back to the hotel and then set out for the office to begin the evening shift. A block from the hotel he was passing the mouth of an alley when he heard someone cry out in pain. The alley was dark, and Shannon could not see what was happening from his position in the sunbathed street. He drew his Colt and started down the passage, pausing only momentarily to let his eyes adjust to the shadows. Ahead of him, a large man was standing over someone lying on the ground. As Shannon drew nearer, the large man kicked the fallen figure viciously in the head, then bent over the unconscious form.

Shannon's eyes narrowed as he saw that the large man was Bo Clagg. As he watched, Clagg reached down and began going through the prostrate man's pockets. He pulled out a few bills and coins, then a watch and chain. Clagg looked at the watch for a moment, then stuffed both watch and money into his own pockets. Satisfied that there was nothing else of value to be taken, Clagg drew back his leg to deliver another kick.

"That's enough, Clagg," Shannon said. "Back away from that man."

Clagg whirled, startled by the interruption. Then he saw who it was, and relaxed with a contemptuous smile on his lips.

"What're you buttin' in for, Shannon?" he growled. "I told you to leave me alone. This saddle bum was drunk and disorderly. I was just arrestin' him."

Shannon pushed Clagg roughly aside and knelt beside the fallen man. As Shannon bent over him, he opened his eyes, moaned, and tried to sit up. Shannon helped him to a sitting position. The man cried out in pain and clutched at his side.

"Just take it easy, mister," Shannon said. "What outfit are you with?"

"Box Y," the man wheezed, feeling his cracked ribs.

Shannon helped the cowman to his feet, then looked coldly at Clagg.

"The money, Clagg," he said. "And the watch. Hand them over."

"I ain't gonna. . . ."

Shannon was now nose to nose with Clagg.

"*Hand them over!*" he shouted.

Cursing and glowering, Clagg dragged the watch and money out of his pocket and slapped them hard into Shannon's outstretched palm. Shannon returned both money and watch to the still-dazed victim.

"Come on, cowboy," Shannon said, taking the man's arm. "I'll get you to a doctor."

"If it's all the same to you, Marshal," said the cowman, "I'd just as soon go on back to my outfit. I want to get out of this town as soon as possible."

"I don't blame you," Shannon said. "I'll borrow a wagon and take you to your camp." He gave Clagg a last withering glare and then helped the injured man out toward the main street.

He borrowed a wagon from the livery stable and drove out to the Box Y encampment, with Clagg's victim lying in the back and the cowboy's horse tied behind. As Shannon drove up, several of the Box Y men, with their foreman, McLean, in the lead, got up and came over to the wagon.

"What's this, Shannon?" McLean asked, helping his rider off the buckboard. "One of you deputies beat up on him?"

"In this case, I'm afraid that's true," Shannon said, untying the Texan's horse and handing the reins to one of his comrades. "I'm sorry. I offered to get him to a doctor, but he wanted to come straight back here."

"Don't blame Marshal Shannon, boss," the injured man said. "He ran the other deputy off and brought me out here. Thanks, Marshal. I'm grateful to you for your help."

Shannon climbed back onto the seat of the wagon. McLean came over to stand beside him.

"I appreciate what you did, Shannon," he said grudgingly. "I guess Kansas lawmen aren't all bad. But the boys are going to be pretty angry about this. I can't guarantee you I'll be able to keep them from coming into town looking for Clagg."

"Tell them the situation is being taken care of," Shannon said, "and warn them not to do anything foolish. We'll deal with Clagg ourselves."

Shannon drove back to town with black rage smouldering in his heart. *How can a man shame himself and his profession like that?* Shannon thought, pushing the horses faster. *He's an insult to every honorable lawman who ever lived, and I'm going to do something about it.*

He found Clagg standing at the bar in a saloon near the spot where Shannon had left him a short time earlier.

"Outside, Bo," Shannon said. Clagg snickered.

"I don't take orders from you, Shannon," he said. "Go find somebody else to preach to."

Shannon stepped forward and placed his nose an inch from Clagg's.

"Outside!" he said. "Now!"

Clagg started to refuse again, but the emotion in Shannon's voice had warned him it was best to comply. He put down his glass and swaggered out the door with Shannon right behind him.

"Awright," Clagg said when they were outside. "What's this all about?"

Shannon shoved Clagg into the mouth of the same alley where he had found him earlier.

"Clagg," he said, "you're through. You're not fit to call yourself a lawman. You're a disgrace to your profession and an embarrassment to everyone who has to work with you. Hand over your badge."

"I ain't givin' you my badge," Clagg said indignantly. "You ain't got no authority to take it, neither. You're only a deputy, just like me."

"Not like you," Shannon said passionately. "Never like you."

"Well, you ain't gettin' my badge. You can't fire me, Shannon, and you know it."

"No," Shannon said, "I can't fire you, but I can give you a choice, and the choice is to either give me that star, or I'll march you straight into Hollister's office. Then you can explain to him assault, robbery, corruption, and whatever else you're guilty of. Hollister doesn't like you any more than I do, and he may not stop with just kicking you off the force. He might decide to throw you into a cell with some of the people you've beaten up."

"Blast your meddlin' hide!" Clagg shouted. "I'll fix you!"

He started to draw his revolver, but before his hand had even touched the handle of the six-gun, Shannon had pulled his own weapon and placed its muzzle against Clagg's forehead, right between the eyes. Clagg froze, astonished by the speed of Shannon's draw.

"Now, Clagg," Shannon said, "since you didn't like the first choice I offered you, I'm going to give you another one. Give me the badge or I'll blow your head off. Resign or die. It's up to you. I don't much care which."

"You wouldn't dare shoot me," Clagg spluttered.

"Are you sure you want to take that chance?" Shannon asked.

Clagg hesitated. Beads of perspiration had appeared on his brow, and he was shaking violently.

"You'll never get away with this," he croaked.

"Maybe not," said Shannon, "but your brains will be splattered all over that wall just the same."

Slowly and deliberately, he cocked the hammer of the Colt. The clicking of the cylinder as it turned was clearly audible over the sound of Clagg's labored breathing.

"Okay!" Clagg cried. "Okay! Here, take the stupid badge. I'm sick of bein' a deputy anyway."

"A wise decision," Shannon said. He took the badge from Clagg's trembling hand and slipped it into his shirt pocket. Then he reached over, extracted Clagg's revolver from his holster, and tossed it into a nearby trash barrel.

"Now get out of my sight," he said. "Go on, *run!*"

Clagg gave him a look of unbridled hatred and shambled off up the alley. As he reached the street, he turned around and shook his fist at Shannon.

"I'll get you for this," he snarled. "I'll get you good."

He lurched around the corner and was gone.

When Shannon entered the marshal's office, he found all of the deputies there except Clagg. Hollister came out of his office with some papers in his hand.

"Okay, boys," he said. "I asked you to come in this afternoon because there are some things I need to go over with you. Where's Clagg?"

Shannon extracted Clagg's badge from his pocket and handed it to Hollister.

"Clagg just resigned," he said. "Here's his star."

Hollister took the badge, puzzled.

"Never figured he'd resign voluntarily," he said. "Why did he quit?"

"I guess he felt there were better career opportunities elsewhere," Shannon said innocently.

Hollister looked keenly at him.

"Something's fishy here," he said. "Did you lean on him?"

"Not exactly," Shannon said. "We just discussed his aptitude for law enforcement while I rested the barrel of my six-gun lightly against his forehead."

Hollister gaped at him. The other deputies guffawed loudly.

"I didn't hear that last part," Hollister said. He looked sharply at the other deputies.

"Nobody else heard it either, right?" he asked.

"What last part?" asked Tucker. "All we heard was that Clagg resigned."

"Well, if he's resigned then that's it, I guess," Hollister said cheerfully, tossing Clagg's badge into a desk drawer. "Can't stop a man from quitting if he wants to. Even our friend Councilman Martz can't object to that. Leaves us short-handed again, though."

"Not really," Tucker said. "We lost Clagg, but we got Shannon. I'd say that was a pretty good trade."

Chapter Fourteen

Clay Shannon moved slowly along the city's main thoroughfare, making his afternoon rounds. Daisy Fisher hove into view and came up to him, her heavily made-up face alight.

"Oh, Clay," she said, "how nice to see you. Why don't we get together at the Emerald Palace tonight? I've got that bottle of champagne cooling in my sitting-room. Will you come?"

"Perhaps," Shannon said, trying desperately to think of something to discourage her. Why wouldn't this silly woman leave him alone?

"Wonderful!" Daisy said. She leaned over and kissed him resoundingly on the cheek. "I'll be waiting for you," she added, winking broadly at him. Shannon edged around her and hastened away, greatly embarrassed.

The embarrassment immediately became worse as

Marian Thomas crossed the street and stepped into his path. The smile she gave him was distinctly chilly.

"A friend of yours, Clay?" she asked, indicating the departing Daisy Fisher.

"No, she's not," Shannon said. "She wants to be, but she isn't."

"Well, then," Marian said with a little sniff, "you'd better wipe your non-friend's lip rouge off your face."

Shannon flushed and rubbed his cheek vigorously with his handkerchief to remove the red smear. Then he clumsily made his excuses and fled, feeling completely humiliated. In his haste to escape, he did not notice the anguish on Marian's face as she watched him go.

Marian went back to the hotel and started to go up to her room. Her father looked out of his office door and greeted her as she went by. Ted Thomas was an elderly man who had married late in life, and Marian, his only child, was his pride and joy. He saw that she was unhappy about something, and came out of the office.

"What's the matter?" he asked, removing the pipe from his mouth.

"Nothing, Dad."

"Hm," Thomas said. He knew his daughter well, and he had noticed the growing friendship between the girl and Clay Shannon. He also recognized the symptoms of a problem of the heart.

"It's that Shannon boy, isn't it?" he asked.

"No," Marian said quickly. "Yes. I don't know."

"You like him, don't you?" Thomas asked.

"I can't help liking him," Marian replied. "He's so different from the rest of the men around here. There's something special about him, Father. He has a kind of quiet strength I can't explain."

The elder Thomas sighed.

"Don't get too fond of that young man, Marian," he said. "He's in a dangerous profession, especially in this town. He has a short life expectancy, and not much in the way of prospects if he does survive."

"I know, Dad," Marian said. "I wish I didn't know it, but I do." She went rapidly up the stairs, her head bowed so her father would not see the tears in her eyes.

Twilight was gathering as Shannon continued his patrol around the city. He was repelled by Daisy Fisher's bold overture and bothered by Marian's reaction to it. He knew that although Marian had not actually said so, she had been distressed by the little scene with Daisy, and this depressed him. His interest in Marian Thomas was growing, and he was very sorry that he had inadvertently hurt her.

As these somber thoughts ran through his mind, he started down the alley that ran along the rear of a number of saloons and other establishments on the main street near the edge of town. He was brought out of his reverie by the sight of a man lying sprawled in the dust ahead of him. He knelt down beside the crumpled figure to investigate. Even in the fading light he could see that the man's eyes were blackened and that there was blood on his face and clothes.

The man realized that Shannon was kneeling next to him and recoiled in fear.

"It's all right, friend," Shannon said. "I'm a city marshal. What happened to you?"

"They picked me clean and then kicked me out, Marshal," he gasped, wiping his sleeve across his bloody nose.

"Who did?" Shannon asked.

"That pack of two-legged wolves in the Yellow Dog Saloon," the man said. "I got into a poker game in there, and before I knew it I was losing real bad. I could see they was cheating me, but when I tried to quit they wouldn't let me. They held a gun on me and made me play until I was flat broke. When they'd taken my last cent, they beat me up and threw me out. One of 'em cut me, too, while they was holding my arms." Shannon looked and saw that there were several long knife slashes across the man's chest. They did not appear to be deep, but they were bleeding and must have been very painful.

"Come on," Shannon said. "There's a doctor right down the street. Let's get you patched up."

While the doctor was working on the injured man, Shannon questioned him more closely, discovering that he was a rider for a cattle outfit that had just arrived in Longhorn that day. He had become separated from his friends and had unwisely wandered alone into the Yellow Dog looking for some entertainment.

"How is he, Doc?" Shannon asked.

"Not too bad," the doctor said. "I don't like the look

of that right eye, though. He took a pretty bad blow there. He could lose it entirely."

Another victim of this terrible town, Shannon thought. *It goes on and on and on, and there's nothing I can do to stop it. Or is there?*

As he was coming out of the doctor's office, he saw Steve Warren patrolling down the other side of the street, and hailed him.

"Steve," he said as they walked together, "what can you tell me about the Yellow Dog Saloon?"

"Worst dive in the city," Warren said, jiggling a store's doorknob to make sure the door was locked. "Every game in the house is rigged, the liquor's watered, and the girls who work there are just like most of the saloon girls in Longhorn, only worse. These young Texas cowhands don't stand a chance in there. If the cowboy has any money left after he's been cheated at the tables, the girls will try to get the kid to spend the rest on fake champagne for them, and if that doesn't work, they'll pick the poor sap's pocket before the bouncers beat him up and toss him out."

"Why don't we shut the place down?"

"My, you are a babe in the woods, aren't you?" Warren asked with a friendly grin. "Well, there are a couple of reasons. First, in Longhorn, cheating cowboys is the universal pastime, and most of the saloons in the city are clip joints. If we started closing them all, Longhorn's economy would suffer, and the city fathers don't want that happening. Second, the Yellow Dog belongs to Rufe Tittle. You know what that means. We can't touch it. City Council would spank us."

Shannon nodded gravely. He had heard of Rufus Tittle. Tittle was a very rich man, one of the city's richest. Like Bo Clagg's cousin Arthur Martz, Tittle was a member of the City Council, and it was common knowledge that he had his fellow councilmen firmly in his pocket. *More dirty politics,* Shannon said to himself. *Another big shot who can't be touched. Supposedly.*

"What's your interest in the Yellow Dog?" Warren asked as they came abreast of the saloon.

Shannon made his decision.

"I'm going to close it," he answered. "Will you watch my back while I go in there?"

"You're crazy, Clay," Warren said in astonishment. "Anybody who tried to close that roach trap would probably find himself face down in a water trough somewhere with a couple of bullets between his shoulder blades. Besides, it wouldn't do any good. The place would just be open again by noon tomorrow. Maybe sooner."

"I'm going to shut it down," Shannon said stubbornly. "Will you back me up or not?"

Warren thought for a moment, then laughed.

"Okay," he said. "I must be crazy too, but I'll back you. What do you want me to do?"

"Just stay here outside the door and make sure nobody comes in behind me."

"You've got it. You sure you want to do this?"

"Yes," Shannon said. He went through the swinging doors, the anger and frustration burning within him.

The Yellow Dog was crowded and noisy. Shannon stood just inside the door, studying the layout of the saloon. The main room was large, with a long bar occupying one wall. Gaming tables were scattered here and there, and a wooden stairway led up to a railed gallery that ran along one side of the second level. Several doors led off the gallery, but they were all closed and Shannon could not tell what lay beyond them. He knew that if trouble started, those doors would bear watching.

He turned his attention to the first floor of the saloon. The air was thick with tobacco smoke, and there was a smell in the air of alcohol, sweat, and horses. The place was crowded with people, and Shannon saw that most of the men were Diamond M hands.

Gradually, as the occupants of the saloon began to notice his presence and his grim expression, an uneasy silence fell upon the room. Soon everyone was staring at Shannon with unfriendly eyes, waiting for him to speak. The bartender sidled out from behind the bar and vanished into a room in the rear. A few seconds later a short man in a frayed frock coat came out, a mixture of irritation and apprehension on his face.

"Yeah, Marshal," he said. "I'm the manager. Whatcha want?"

"Do you have a chain and padlock handy?" Shannon asked blandly.

"Huh? Well, yeah, I got a padlock in the back somewhere," the manager said, perplexed. "Why?"

"Because this establishment is closed," Shannon said. "Immediately, and until further notice."

The manager's jaw dropped and he goggled uncomprehendingly at Shannon.

"*What?*" he cried. "Closed? Whaddaya mean, *closed?*"

"Closed means closed," Shannon said, "as in shut down, cleared out, and locked up. Now."

"You can't do that," the manager said indignantly.

"I just did," Shannon said.

"Do you know who owns this saloon?" the manager sputtered. "Rufe Tittle will have your hide. You're going to be in a lot of trouble, pal."

"I'll chance it," Shannon said. "Meanwhile, *pal,* you've got five minutes to run everybody out of here and get the doors padlocked. Otherwise, you're going to jail, so you'd better get moving."

On the sidewalk, Deputy Marshal Warren watched with amusement as angry men began coming out of the saloon. They glared at Warren and began drifting away along the street, growling and cursing

Walt Tucker came along the boardwalk and greeted Warren.

"What's going on?" he asked.

"Shannon's closing the place," Warren replied.

"What? Why is he doing that?"

"I don't know. I guess he just wants to. He's apparently pretty riled up about something that went on in there earlier tonight."

"Well, well," Tucker said, rubbing his chin. "This should be interesting."

After the former customers of the Yellow Dog had all had drifted away, the lights began to go out in the saloon one by one, and shortly thereafter the manager came out holding a lock and a short length of chain. Shannon followed him out and stood watchfully by as the doors of the saloon were closed and secured. The manager then trotted off, mumbling imprecations to himself.

"Hello, Walt," Shannon said to Tucker. "Everything quiet tonight?"

"Yeah," Tucker said, "but it won't be for long when word of this gets around."

The three deputies went back to the office. Marshal Hollister was still there, working at his desk, and Shannon told him what he had done. Hollister stared at him in surprise for a moment, then began to laugh.

"That should put a burr under Rufe Tittle's saddle," he said. "I'll bet he's going to be foaming at the mouth when he hears about this. It'll be a pleasure to hear him holler. But it won't stick, Clay. Tittle will be in here by eight o'clock tomorrow morning with a court order reopening the place."

The deputies all gathered in the office early the next morning, drinking coffee and waiting for the inevitable. At precisely 7:55 Councilman Rufus Tittle came storming into the office, looking like a thundercloud and bellowing like a dyspeptic ox.

"Hollister," he shouted, "did you order the Yellow Dog to be closed?"

"Nope," Hollister said.

"Then why was it shut down last night?"

"Well, for one thing, one of my deputies discovered that some of the gaming tables in there were just a wee bit crooked. Bet that comes as a big shock to you, doesn't it, Rufe?"

Tittle swore and waved a folded paper at Hollister. "This is a court order requiring the saloon to be reopened immediately and prohibiting you and your deputies from interfering with its operations," Tittle said. "This better not happen again, Hollister, or Longhorn will be looking for a new city marshal." He glared at Shannon. "Don't cross my trail again, boy," he said. "Nobody messes with me in this town, and you'd better remember that."

He threw the court order down on Hollister's desk and went out, still fuming.

Hollister picked up the paper and deposited it in a handy wastebasket.

"Come on into my office, Clay," Hollister said. "We need to talk."

They went into the inner office, and Hollister closed the door.

"I've got to admire your guts, Clay," he said, "but one lesson a good lawman learns early is that he can't afford to let anger affect his judgment. In our line of work we see a lot of bad things, things so terrible they make any decent man want to do something to stop them. But when you wear a badge you have to keep your temper, and when you take action it must be purposeful and effective. There's no place in this business for useless gestures. They accomplish nothing and often they just make things worse."

Shannon squirmed uncomfortably. He saw now that he had let his righteous indignation get the better of his common sense. He was not concerned for himself, but it bothered him greatly that his precipitous act might have placed his fellow deputies in danger, or created difficulties for Marshal Hollister, who had been kind enough to give him his deputy's badge.

"I hope I haven't gotten you into trouble, too, Marshal," Shannon said.

"Not to amount to anything," Hollister said. "Despite Tittle's threats, City Council won't dare touch me. I've got friends too. Otherwise, I wouldn't have kept this job as long as I have. Anyway, the Yellow Dog will be going full blast by midday, and Tittle will cool off once the money starts rolling in again."

"I guess it was all for nothing, then," Shannon said dejectedly.

Hollister patted him on the shoulder.

"Don't let it bother you too much, son," he said. "I know how you feel, but neither you nor I can change this town. All we can do is try to keep a lid on it. But watch your back from now on, Clay. You're making some powerful enemies."

"I'll be careful," Shannon promised.

"Good," Hollister said. "Now let's get back to work, shall we?"

Shannon went out of the office, vowing that never again would he let his emotions cloud his judgment as a law officer. It was, he reflected, an embarrassing but valuable lesson, and one he would not forget. Clay Shannon had taken another step on the long, hard road to wisdom.

Chapter Fifteen

The next day was quiet, or at least as quiet as Longhorn ever got. Shannon sat in a chair in front of the marshal's office, thinking of Marian Thomas. He had seen her several times since the encounter on the street with Daisy Fisher, but she had not mentioned the incident again. However, he had noticed that there was now a certain somberness in her dark brown eyes when she looked at him, as if she was gazing into the future and was saddened by what she saw.

For several days he had been eating supper in the restaurant near the marshal's office, because he did not like to be away from the office too long as darkness approached. Evening was Longhorn's busiest time, and therefore the busiest time for the city's lawmen as well. On this particular evening, however, there seemed to be a lull in Longhorn's usual frantic pace, and so Shannon decided to go back to the hotel to have supper in the dining room. The food was better there, he told himself, and if he was lucky the company might be better too.

His optimism was rewarded. Business was slow in the dining room, and Marian Thomas sat with him as he ate.

"I hear you closed up the Yellow Dog Saloon," she said.

"It didn't do any good," Shannon said morosely.

"I hope it doesn't do any harm," she replied. "To any of us."

Shannon paused, his fork halfway to his mouth.

"Why should it harm you?" he asked.

"My father only runs this hotel," she replied. "Rufus Tittle owns it."

Shannon put down the fork. The consequences of his hasty act the previous evening seemed to be spreading like ripples on a pond.

"I'm sorry if I've caused you any difficulty," he said. "Perhaps I'd better find a room somewhere else."

"Please don't," Marian said. "I'd rather you stayed here."

"Why?" Shannon asked.

"You're the only one in town who likes my cooking," she said, blushing.

Shannon picked up the fork again.

"Of course," he said. "What other reason could there be?"

The next day Shannon was eating lunch in the restaurant near the marshal's office when Packy Flynn, one of the jailers, came running in.

"Shannon!" the jailer said breathlessly. "I been

lookin' for somebody and there's no one in the office. Bonham's in a jam."

Shannon pushed back his chair, tossed a coin on the table to pay for the half-eaten meal, and followed the jailer out the door.

"He's at the schoolhouse," Packy said. "A bunch of them Diamond M toughs have got him cornered. One of the kids from the school came to the office to report it."

"What was Cash doing in the schoolhouse?" Shannon asked, striding along beside the agitated jailer.

"I dunno," Packy said, still trying to catch his breath. "He's been courtin' the schoolmarm for the last coupla months. Maybe he went down there to see her."

As they approached the schoolhouse, they saw that a number of children were gathered out in front, huddled together in obvious fright. The schoolteacher broke away from the group and came running to meet Shannon.

"Hurry!" she said. "Cash is in there. You've got to help him."

"What's going on?" Shannon asked.

"Four of those awful cow people broke into the classroom just as I was about to dismiss the class. They were drunk, and they kept yelling at us to get out because they were going to burn down the school. I took the children outside immediately."

"How did Bonham get involved?" Shannon asked, slipping the rawhide loop off the hammer of his six-gun.

"He often comes by in the afternoon to see me," the teacher said, her cheeks coloring slightly. "Today when he got here I told him what had happened. He went right inside and hasn't come out again. I'm afraid for him. There were a lot of those Texas people, and they were in an ugly mood."

Shannon went up to one of the school's front windows and looked in. Cash Bonham was seated comfortably on the edge of the teacher's desk, surrounded by four Diamond M riders, three of whom had six-guns in their hands. Bonham was speaking calmly to them, but Shannon could see that his words were not having much effect. The fourth cowman was holding a lighted oil lamp. The oil splashed out of the lamp as the man waved it recklessly around.

"Is there a back door to this place?" Shannon asked the schoolteacher.

"Yes," she said. "It opens directly into the classroom. What are you going to do?"

"I don't know," Shannon said, "but from the looks of things, I'd better do it pretty soon."

He told the teacher to take the children and leave the area so none of them would be hurt if there was shooting. Only the jailer, Packy Flynn, remained behind, watching Shannon expectantly.

"You staying?" Shannon asked.

"Bet your life," Packy said. "I wouldn't miss this for nothin'."

"Then keep out of sight and try not to get any holes in you. By the time this is over, we may need all the jailers we've got."

Shannon went around to the rear of the building and stopped by the back door, listening to the angry voices being raised inside the school. He slid the Colt back into his holster, then carefully eased the door open and stepped through it. He found himself in the classroom, standing just a few feet behind the teacher's desk, where Bonham was still sitting in apparent unconcern. The cowboys grouped around the desk jumped nervously as Shannon entered. They raised their six-guns, then hesitated as they saw that Shannon was empty-handed. Bonham did not even turn around, because he had seen Shannon looking in the window and knew who it was behind him.

"Hello, Cash," Shannon said easily. "Entertaining some new students, I see."

"Afternoon, Clay," Bonham said, rolling himself a cigarette. "Yes, these fellows came to visit class today. Seems like they have some sort of grudge against places of learning. Against places of worship too, I gather. These are the same ones who burned down the church last year."

"You keep your hands in sight and don't try nothing, Shannon," the cowman standing at the front of the pack snarled. "Yeah, we made a bonfire out of that hallelujah joint last year, and now we're gonna leave you a little souvenir of this year's trail drive too."

Bonham started to put the cigarette to his lips. Immediately, the Diamond M men covered him with their six-guns.

"You just watch what you're doing there, Bonham," the first cowhand said. "We know your reputation with those guns of yours. I met a cowpoke down Tascosa way a few months ago, and he told me you was the fastest gun he'd ever seen. Well, your fast draw ain't gonna do you any good this time. Even you can't beat four men who've already got the drop on you."

Bonham struck a match on his boot sole and lit his cigarette. Shannon saw that his hand was as steady as a rock while he did it. *What nerves,* Shannon thought to himself. *Four drunks about to shoot him, and he's as cool as ice.*

"I've been trying to explain to these gentlemen that burning down schoolhouses is not an approved activity, even in Longhorn," Bonham said, blowing a smoke ring at the ceiling. "Unfortunately, they seem determined to ignore my wise counsel."

"Yeah, gunslinger," another of the Diamond M men said. "We got a score to settle with this town and with you tin stars too. You give us any lip, and we'll burn you right along with the schoolhouse. Both of you."

Bonham stood up slowly, yawning. As he rose, he caught Shannon's eye.

"I'm afraid we're not going to be able to settle this amicably," he said casually. "Too bad."

"Yes, it's a pity," said Shannon, bracing himself. He knew what Bonham was going to do.

"That's enough talk," the first Diamond M man said. "Ike, toss that lamp."

The cowhand with the oil lamp cocked his arm to hurl it at the desk. Bonham and Shannon moved simultaneously. Bonham's hands were a blur as they went under his coat, and before the Texas men could react they found themselves covered by both Bonham's twin six-guns and Shannon's Colt. The cowpunchers froze, unable to believe the suddenness with which the two lawmen had turned the tables on them.

"Decision time, gents," Bonham said. "You with the oil lamp . . . if your arm starts forward, you're a dead man. Understand? The rest of you . . . do you want to live or die? If you decide you'd rather live, uncock those six-guns and put them on the floor, nice and easy."

The Diamond M men looked at each other and then gingerly placed their weapons on the floor. One of them gave a low whistle.

"I don't believe it!" he said. "I never even saw their hands move!"

"Yeah," another said. "Mike, whoever you talked to in Tascosa was right. Only he forgot to mention there was two of these Kansas star-packers who could draw like that."

"When you're through admiring Kansas efficiency," Bonham said, "just turn around and march out of here with your hands high. I think the judge will want to have a little talk with you."

When the Diamond M men were locked in their cells, Bonham and Shannon came back into the office. Hollister, Tucker, and Warren were gathered there, listening with great interest as Packy excitedly related the confrontation in the schoolhouse. He had seen it all through the classroom window, and he could hardly contain his exhilaration.

"Yessir," he said. "Four of 'em had the drop on Cash and Shannon, and our boys covered 'em before they could pull a trigger. Why, Shannon had his gun on 'em as fast as Cash, maybe even a little faster."

"Well, Bonham," Hollister said, "looks like you've

got a rival for the quick-draw championship of Long-horn."

"Yeah," Tucker said with a twinkle in his eye. "That bother you any, Cash?"

Bonham chuckled.

"Nope," he said. "Once it might have, but not any more."

He smiled sardonically at Shannon.

"One thing I've learned over the years," he said, lighting another cigarette, "is that no matter how fast you are, sooner or later somebody will come along who's faster. There's no use getting bent out of shape about it. That's just the way life is. Congratulations, Clay. You did a good job in there. That situation could have gotten pretty nasty, and I'm mighty glad you came along. It took some guts to walk in there like you did. Thanks for backing me up."

He reached out to shake Shannon's hand. Shannon, abashed, could only take the proffered hand and grin sheepishly.

"Marshal," Bonham said, turning to Hollister, "you've got a good man here. I suggest you hang onto him."

"I will," said Hollister, beaming at Shannon. "At least until someone who's faster than he is comes along."

"Don't hold your breath," Bonham said. "That might be awhile."

It dawned suddenly on Shannon that in his brief time in Longhorn, he had somehow and in some small measure earned the respect of these four lawmen. At that moment in his young life, nothing could have meant more to him, or given him greater satisfaction.

Chapter Sixteen

It was late the next evening when Shannon finished writing out his daily report and leaned back in his office chair. He glanced at the pendulum clock on the wall and saw that it was nearly 11:00. He had the night shift, so it would be many hours before he would be able to go back to the hotel and sleep. Steve Warren was in the office, preparing to go off duty.

"Hey, Shannon," he said, "I hear our friend Bo Clagg has joined up with the Diamond M."

"I guess that's not too surprising," Shannon said. "He ought to fit right in with that gang. Well, their loss is our gain. I'd say they deserved each other."

Daisy Fisher came flouncing into the office.

"Hello, Daisy," Warren said. "What brings you to this den of righteousness?"

"A man just insulted me out there," Daisy said indignantly. "A lady isn't safe on streets in this town anymore."

"You're safe anywhere, Daisy," Warren said with a wink at Shannon.

"No, I'm not," Daisy said. "It's very late, and I'm afraid to go out there again alone. I want Clay to escort me back to the Emerald Palace."

Warren looked at Shannon with ill-concealed glee.

"It's your duty to assist the lady, Clay," he said with mock solemnity. "Our job is to protect the public. Besides, you have to go out anyway. It's time for the eleven o'clock rounds."

Shannon sighed and rose from his chair.

Self-consciously, he walked beside Daisy Fisher toward the Emerald Palace Saloon. Daisy was clinging tightly to his arm and smiling proudly at the people passing by. She smelled of cheap perfume, and her heavy makeup was visible even in the semi-darkness of the boardwalk. Shannon uttered a silent prayer that they would not encounter Marian Thomas again. He tried to pull away from Daisy's clutching hands, but her grip on his arm was too tight.

"What's the matter, Clay?" she asked plaintively. "Don't you like me? You and I could have some good times together, you know."

Shannon searched desperately for some way to discourage the woman without hurting her feelings.

"Miss Daisy," he said, "I. . . ."

He was interrupted by the pounding of approaching hooves, and a volley of gunshots shattered the evening. Three horsemen came charging around the next corner at a full gallop, firing their revolvers left and right.

"Get down!" Shannon shouted, pushing Daisy Fisher away from him and drawing his six-gun. As the riders came abreast of Shannon, one of them whooped "Look, boys! One of them Yankee law dogs!" All three men turned in the saddle and fired at Shannon as they galloped by. First one bullet, then another sang past Shannon's ear. Daisy Fisher uttered a grunt of surprise and sat down heavily on the sidewalk.

The horsemen were past them now, still shooting back at them. Shannon ran into the street. Raising the Colt, he took careful aim and fired. One of the riders cursed and dropped his six-gun. Shannon fired again, and a second rider lurched in his saddle. The man riding alongside him reached over and held him upright as they all turned another corner and disappeared from view.

Cash Bonham arrived, revolver at the ready.

"What was all the noise about?" he asked.

"Three cowboys came by, shooting up the town," Shannon said, holstering his weapon. He knew it was no use trying to follow the men. He was on foot, and they would be well away before he could retrieve his horse from the livery stable. "They tried to plug me," he added, "but their aim was bad. I think I winged a couple of them."

"Did you see who they were?" Bonham asked.

"Yes," Shannon said. "They passed right through the light from the lamp post there. The horses had Diamond M brands."

"That bunch of hooligans again," Bonham said. "I'll be glad when they leave Longhorn for good."

They went back to the boardwalk. Daisy Fisher was

still lying where she had fallen. As Shannon bent over to help her up, he saw with horror the dark stain of blood beside her.

"She's been shot!" he said, raising her head and shoulders off the rough boards. "We've got to get her to a doctor."

Cash Bonham knelt beside him.

"No point in that," he said quietly.

Daisy Fisher opened her eyes and looked at Shannon.

"You're a nice boy, Clay," she said. "You and I could have. . . ."

Her voice trailed off and her body went limp in Shannon's arms. Shannon eased her gently down onto the walk. He fought back the rage that was rising in him, remembering his vow never again to let his emotions influence his professional judgment.

"Take care of her, will you, Cash?" he asked in a hollow voice.

"Sure," Bonham said. "Where are you headed?"

"I'm going to wake up that half-witted judge of ours. I want three John Doe warrants for murder, and I want them fast."

"Don't take it so hard, Clay," Bonham said. "She was just another saloon girl, and a considerably over-aged one at that."

"I know what she was," Shannon said coldly. "But she was a human being, too. She had as much right to live as anyone else. Tell Marshal Hollister I've gone to get those warrants."

Shannon came striding into the marshal's office

twenty minutes later. Hollister, Tucker, and Bonham were there, waiting.

"You get the warrants?" Hollister asked him. Shannon held up the folded papers.

"That was record time," Warren said. "Judge Hester must be more obliging than usual tonight. Or less drunk."

"He was drunk, all right," Shannon said. "I told him the three men had sworn to kill him, and if he didn't issue the warrants immediately so we could arrest them, they'd come back to get him. I hope he doesn't remember that fairy tale when he wakes up in the morning."

He lifted a rifle down from the rack on the wall and checked to see that it was loaded.

"Take Tucker and Bonham with you," Hollister said. "You're going to be outnumbered when you get to the Diamond M camp, so watch yourselves."

The three deputies rode out to the grove of trees beyond the stockyards where the Diamond M crew was camped. As they approached the campfire beside the chuck wagon, they saw that at least a dozen of the Diamond M riders were squatting around the fire, drinking coffee and watching the lawmen's approach with hostile eyes.

"Where are they?" Tucker demanded as they reined up.

"Where's who?" one of the men growled.

"Shannon," Tucker said, "check their horses."

Shannon rode over to the picket line where the Diamond M's horses were tethered. Three of the animals were sweating and quite evidently tired.

"They're here, all right," Shannon said, rejoining the others. As he passed the chuck wagon he heard a scuffling sound inside it. He slid his rifle out of the saddle scabbard and pointed it at the wagon.

"You in the chuck wagon," he said loudly. "Come on out, and come out with your fists empty."

The Diamond M men gathered around the fire stood up, their hands moving close to their holsters as they stared belligerently at Shannon, Tucker, and Bonham.

"Last chance," Shannon called. "Either you come out, or I start putting holes in the side of the wagon."

Three men climbed slowly down from the chuck wagon. One was supporting a second man; the third had a bloody bandana wrapped around his forearm.

"Let's go, boys," Tucker said. "It's a long walk back to town."

"You ain't takin' *nobody* to town," a tall cowhand yelled, touching the handle of his six-gun. The other Diamond M men stepped forward, reaching for their weapons.

"Back off!" Cash Bonham said, covering them with his revolver. "These coyotes are under arrest for murder, and anybody who tries to interfere is going to get slightly shot."

"Cut 'em down, boys!" the tall Diamond M man shouted, starting to pull his six-gun.

Cash Bonham fanned off three quick shots from his revolver. Dirt spurted up around the feet of the advancing Texans.

"Next one goes in your gut, mister," Tucker said, pointing his rifle at the tall cowpuncher's midsection. "Now back off, all of you, or take your medicine."

There was a rumble of discontent from the trail herders, but they let their revolvers slip back into their holsters.

"Start walking, you miserable slime," Shannon said, prodding one of Daisy Fisher's killers in the back with the muzzle of his rifle. "And don't hesitate to try to get away if you feel lucky. I'd like nothing better than to shoot you down in the road. Just give me an excuse."

Cautiously, the deputies backed their horses away from the fire, and then, still watching over their shoulders, they rode away toward Longhorn, the three cowmen stumbling disconsolately ahead of them.

The next morning Cliff Horrocks, the Diamond M's surly foreman, came stalking into the marshal's office. Shannon and Warren were at their desks.

"I been in town all night," Horrocks said, glowering at Shannon. "I just heard you jailed three of my boys."

"You hear good," Warren said.

"I don't like my people being tossed in jail," Horrocks said belligerently.

"Then keep them under control," Shannon snapped. "A woman was killed last night, and your men are going to stand trial for murder. Don't let that sort of thing happen again, Horrocks, or we'll throw the whole bunch of you into the cells and let you rot there."

"Yeah, well, you hate Texans, don't you, Shannon?" Horrocks asked.

"No," Shannon replied. "I just hate some of the

things you do. Last warning, Horrocks. Keep your pack of mongrels under control, or we will."

When Horrocks had left, Shannon went to the door and watched him until he was out of sight.

"I hope we don't have any more trouble with them," Warren said.

"So do I," Shannon said. "So do I."

But it was not to be.

Chapter Seventeen

Shannon had just returned to the office from lunch when one of the bartenders from the Yellow Dog Saloon ran in.

"Come quick!" he cried. "There's a gunfight in the Yellow Dog."

"Who's fighting?" Shannon asked.

"Some of the Box Y men came into the saloon, and there was a lot of yelling and cussing between them and the Diamond M riders. One of the Diamond M people pulled a gun on a Box Y hand."

Shannon and Warren started for the Yellow Dog. As they came through the swinging doors, they saw that a Box Y man was sprawled on the floor, bleeding from a gunshot wound to the face.

A Diamond M rider was standing over him, holding a six-gun.

"I'll fix you!" the Diamond M man shouted, pointing the pistol at the fallen man.

Shannon leaped between the gunman and his intended victim.

"Hold it!" he said. "This man's down and he's not even armed."

"Get outta the way," the Diamond M cowhand said, "or I'll gun you too."

He cocked the pistol, and his knuckles whitened as he started to squeeze the trigger.

"Look out, Clay!" Warren shouted.

Almost without conscious thought, Shannon drew and fired. The Diamond M man staggered backwards and sprawled on the floor, his pistol bouncing a dozen feet away.

A roar went up from the other Diamond M hands. They drew their six-guns, and the rest of the Box Y men did likewise. For a moment the saloon was on the brink of an all-out gun battle. Fortunately for everyone concerned, at that instant Tucker and Bonham arrived. Tucker was armed with a shotgun, and he began to swing the twin muzzles from one group of cowmen to the other, holding both sides at bay. Warren briefly explained to the two deputies what had occurred.

"Clay fired in self-defense," he said. "That skunk lying on the floor there was going to kill him."

Bonham bent over the downed Diamond M man.

"He's done," he said.

The Box Y cowhand was still alive, and Tucker ordered the other Box Y riders to carry him to the doctor's office. They departed, casting black looks back at the Diamond M men. The undertaker was then summoned to attend to the corpse of the man Shannon had killed.

When the deputies returned to the office, Shannon sank down heavily in a chair, a little shaken by the sudden confrontation that had forced him to take another man's life. He wondered darkly if he would ever get used to shooting people. He concluded that he probably would not.

"We're really going to have trouble with the Diamond M now," Warren said.

"We'll have trouble with the Box Y, too," Shannon said. "The only question is whether they'll come after us or after each other."

Marshal Hollister came out of his office.

"We've got to tell the Diamond M," he said. "It's better that they find out from us than from somebody else. Come on, Clay, let's ride out there and get it over with."

They retrieved their horses from the livery stable and set out for the Diamond M camp. Not surprisingly, the Diamond M hands were less than pleased with the news that one of their own had been killed. Their foreman, Cliff Horrocks, was particularly vocal.

"Who shot him?" Horrocks bawled. "That ex-owlhoot gunfighter Bonham? Shorty wouldn't have had a chance against that killer."

"Bonham didn't shoot him. I did," Shannon said. He explained the circumstances, trying to ignore the murderous stares that were being directed at him.

"You told me to keep my men under control, Shannon," Horrocks said. "I can't promise you anything after this. We've about had it with that Box Y bunch, and with you Kansas law dogs too for that matter. You've pushed us too far."

"Just be sure you don't push *us* too far," Hollister said. "If you come into town looking for trouble, we'll be waiting."

"Tell me something, Horrocks," Shannon said, leaning on his saddle horn. "Have you by any chance seen my friend Bo Clagg recently?"

Horrocks's expression became crafty.

"Clagg?" he asked. "Naw, I ain't seen him at all. Why?"

"I heard a rumor that he might have joined up with your outfit after he retired from the law enforcement business. Seemed a little strange, considering the way you feel about Kansas lawmen."

"I ain't seen him, I said," Horrocks mumbled, averting his eyes.

Shannon nodded.

"I believe you," he said. "Really, I do."

When they returned to the office they found Bonham sitting in one of the chairs out front, looking very unhappy.

"What's wrong, Cash?" Hollister asked.

"It's those four Diamond M people we nailed at the schoolhouse," Bonham said. "Judge Hester turned them loose. 'Lack of evidence,' he said. A little money under the table, more likely."

"Marvelous," Hollister said. "Another glorious victory for the forces of law and order."

"Yeah," Bonham said, "and now we'll have to arrest

them all over again for something else. Makes you wonder why we even bother, doesn't it?"

At sunrise the next day, Shannon was sitting alone in the marshal's office, drinking his first cup of coffee. A man came scurrying in, his cheeks pale. Shannon recognized him as the owner of one of the town's general stores.

"M-M-Marshal," the storekeeper said to Shannon, his lip trembling, "I was just walking past that livery stable up the street, and something terrible's happened there. You'd better take a look."

Shannon followed the agitated storekeeper the hundred yards to the livery stable. He tried to find out what the problem was, but the man kept insisting that Shannon had to come and see for himself.

As they reached the livery stable, the storekeeper stopped, motioning for Shannon to go on.

"I'll wait here," he said. "I don't want to go in there again."

Shannon moved cautiously through the open door of the livery stable. With the morning sun still low in the sky, the interior of the stable was dark, but Shannon could see something in the shadows ahead of him. He stepped closer and looked up. The body of a man was hanging from a rope that had been passed over one of the beams. The storekeeper had not exaggerated. It was a terrible sight.

Shannon had never seen a hanged man before, and his stomach turned over. He fumbled for his pocket knife and cut the rope, letting the body down carefully onto the sawdust of the stable floor. The stable owner came from the street, a toothpick stuck in his mouth.

"What's this?" he asked, nearly swallowing the toothpick as he saw the dead man on his floor.

"Just a slight case of homicide," Shannon said. "Where have you been?"

"Gettin' some breakfast before I came over here. You think he might have killed himself?"

"Not unless he tied his own hands behind his back first. You know him?"

The stable owner bent down to get a better view of the corpse.

"Yeah, he's one of them Box Y people. He left his horse here yesterday afternoon."

Shannon told him to throw a blanket over the body while he went back to the marshal's office to report the death. As he hurried toward the office, his mind preoccupied by what he had just seen, he passed one of the many alleys that ran off the main street. There was a burst of flame from the mouth of the alley, and the blast of a gunshot reverberated from the walls of the surrounding buildings. Shannon felt a searing pain along his side. He flung himself down full length on the ground and rolled back against the front wall of one of the buildings, drawing his six-gun. He could hear footsteps running away down the alley, and he leaped up to follow. As he rushed into the alley, he could see a shadowy figure fleeing ahead of him. Pausing in his flight, the man turned and fired again at Shannon. The bullet passed close to Shannon's head, but he hardly noticed it. In the light of the muzzle flash he had recognized the would-be assassin. It was Bo Clagg.

Shannon fired twice in midstride, but without apparent effect. Clagg merely ran faster, disappearing quickly around a corner ahead of him. When Shannon reached the spot, there was no one to be seen in any direction.

Tucker and Bonham came running in from the main street, their weapons drawn.

"We heard the shots," Tucker said. "What's going on?"

"Bo Clagg just tried to put a couple of holes in me," Shannon said. "He got away before I could return the favor." He touched his burning ribs. His shirt was torn and when he removed his hand there was blood on it.

"You're hurt," Bonham said. "Is it bad?"

"No," Shannon said, "just a crease. We've got bigger things to worry about right now. Somebody left us a little present hanging in the livery stable back there."

He took the other deputies back to the stable and showed them the corpse. Tucker gave a soft whistle.

"Box Y, eh?" he said. "Now the fat's really in the fire. The Box Y boys will blame it on Diamond M. Think Clagg was in on it?"

"I don't know," Shannon said, pressing a handkerchief against his bleeding side. "I suspect he's on the Diamond M payroll now, and I certainly wouldn't put something like this past him."

He drew the blanket back over the dead man.

"Now that I think about it," he continued, "Clagg would have known that somebody would report the lynching, and he might also have known that I was the only one in the office this morning. He's got a big grudge against me, and he may have waited to get a shot at me when I came by on the way to the stable. It's just a guess, though. We've got no proof."

"It's probably a good guess," Tucker said. "Come on, let's get you over to the doc's so he can repair the damage. Looks like you just used up another of your nine lives, son."

They left Shannon at the doctor's office and went back to retrieve the corpse they had left at the livery stable. As the doctor finished applying a bandage to Shannon's side, Marshal Hollister came in. In response to his question, Shannon assured him that the wound was only superficial, and that he was still fit for duty.

"Tucker and Bonham have taken the body over to the undertaker's," Hollister said, "and I've sent word to the Box Y camp. They'll be out for blood after this."

Shannon returned with Hollister to the undertaker's place of business. As they arrived, Lon McLean and several other Box Y men rode up. They dismounted and went into the undertaker's, their faces set and angry. McLean came up to Hollister and Shannon.

"It was the Diamond M, wasn't it?" McLean asked.

"We don't know that," Hollister replied.

"You may not know it, but I do," McLean said. "The man you found hanged was mixed up in that ruckus with the Diamond M people the other night at the Yellow Dog Saloon. It was them, all right. What happened to you, Shannon?" he added, looking at

Shannon's bloodied shirt. Shannon told him about Clagg.

"Yeah," McLean said, "I heard he joined up with the M. Ambushing somebody would be just his style."

The Box Y men came out of the undertaker's muttering among themselves.

"The Diamond M's gonna pay for this," one of them said, glaring at the two lawmen. We're gonna take care of them, and you deputies had better stay out of the way. This is personal between the M and us."

Shannon and Hollister spent several minutes trying to calm them down, but to no avail. The Box Y men mounted their horses and rode furiously away. McLean climbed into his saddle and prepared to follow them.

"Jimmy's right, Hollister," he said. "This is Box Y's affair now. Keep your men out of it, if you don't want them to get caught in the middle."

"Seems to me we're always in the middle," Shannon said, watching him ride off.

"Naturally," Hollister said. "That's what we get paid for."

They spent the remainder of the day searching for anyone who might have seen the hanging or have any other information that would provide a clue to the identity of the hangmen, but their efforts were in vain.

"Let's try the Yellow Dog," Tucker said finally. "Some of the Diamond M people are probably in there. They won't admit to anything, but maybe we can pick up something that will help."

Several of the Diamond M hands were indeed in the

saloon, the foreman, Horrocks, among them. As expected, when Tucker and Shannon questioned them, they all denied having any knowledge of the murder of the Box Y man, but Shannon saw their self-satisfied smiles even as they uttered their denials. *They did it,* Shannon thought to himself. *As sure as the turning of the earth, they did it.*

"What's the matter with your side, Shannon?" Horrocks said with a malevolent leer. "Did a horse bite you?"

"This particular horse was named Clagg," Shannon said, "and I'm willing to bet he's wearing the Diamond M brand on his rump these days. But of course you wouldn't know anything about that, would you?"

"Not me," Horrocks said smugly. "I've been in here playing poker all day."

"Really?" Tucker said. "I've never heard that one before."

As night fell, Marshal Hollister assembled all of the deputies in his office.

"This thing with the Texans is starting to get out of control," he said. "We're going to have trouble. Lots of it, and probably soon. I want you boys to sleep in the office for the next few nights."

"We can't hide in here forever, Bob," Tucker said.

"We're not hiding," Hollister said firmly. "We'll still do our jobs, make our rounds, and try to keep the peace, but when we're not on the street I want all of you right here where I can find you in a hurry. We'll turn the drunks loose and use the bunks in the cells. I'll get Zeke and Packy to clean up the place for us."

"You're staying here too?" Bonham asked. Hollister nodded.

"What about your wife?" Tucker asked. "She won't like being left alone."

"I'm sending her to visit her mother in Wichita," Hollister replied. "This town could blow wide open, and if it does, at least I'll know she's safe."

"Before tonight's over, we may all wish we were in Wichita," Tucker said.

Shannon came down the stairs to the hotel lobby carrying his rifle and saddlebags. Marian Thomas was behind the desk.

"Where are you going?" she asked, frowning.

Shannon explained that Hollister wanted the deputies to spend the night in the office.

"There's going to be serious trouble, isn't there?" she asked in a small voice.

"Probably," Shannon said.

"But you won't run away from it, will you?"

"When you carry the star," Shannon replied, "you don't run away. Ever."

"Why not?" she asked. "This prairie Gomorrah isn't worth your life."

Shannon put down the rifle and saddlebags and took both her hands in his.

"Marian," he said patiently, "you don't understand. When you put on this badge you take on an obligation—to the town, however undeserving it may be— but even more so to yourself. A lawman who runs from trouble isn't a lawman. He ought to take up some other line of work, because he's a disgrace to himself and everyone else who wears the star."

"That's ridiculous," Marian said, pulling her hands away and averting her head.

Shannon waited a moment longer, trying to think of something else to say. Then, defeated by the girl's angry silence, he reluctantly picked up his gear and left the hotel.

Marian's father came out of the his office.

"You look unhappy, my dear," he said. "Did you have an argument with Clay?"

"No," she replied. "Just a discussion. I tried to get him to quit, and he wouldn't. He said I didn't understand, that he has an obligation to stay on. Well, he's right. I don't understand. What's so special about that old badge, anyway? It's just a piece of tin."

Her father smiled sadly at her.

"Yes," he said, "it's just a piece of tin, but Clay's heart is behind it, and that's the problem. He's a fine young man, Marian, but you'd better forget about him. His first love will always be the law."

Chapter Eighteen

As darkness fell, Longhorn's police force gathered in Hollister's office.

"We're going to have to be careful out there to-night," Hollister said. "We'll work in pairs, and we'd all better keep awake if we want to see the sunrise. Shannon, you and Warren. Bonham, you and me. Walt, stay here and hold the fort. Zeke and Packy will both be here, watching the cells while you man the office."

Tucker looked annoyed.

"I don't want to sit around on my backside while the rest of you are out there playing clay pigeon," he said. "Zeke and Packy can take care of the office as well as the jail."

"Sorry," Hollister said. "I want a deputy in here all evening. We're still holding those three skunks who killed Daisy Fisher, and the Diamond M crowd might try to break them out tonight. I need a steady man standing by to handle things if that happens. Besides, I've seen you gimping around since that drunk kicked you yesterday. You can't chase anybody with a game leg, and we may be chasing people tonight. Or running from them. So stay here. Issue shotguns to Zeke and Packy, and keep an eye on the street. If you see anything brewing, send one of the jailers to get us."

Tucker snorted in disgust, but made no further protest.

"Let's go," Hollister said to the others. "Remember to stay together and keep your eyes open."

Warren shook his head in mock dismay.

"My mother wanted me to be a dentist," he said. "Too bad I didn't listen to her."

Shannon and Steve Warren moved carefully along the main street, watching the shadows for any sign of movement. As they passed opposite the Yellow Dog Saloon, they found a store's front door unlocked.

"We'd better check the back door," Shannon said.

Warren leaned against the wall of the store.

"Go ahead," he said. "I'll watch the front."

"Hollister said for us to stay together," said Shannon doubtfully.

"It'll be all right," Warren said. "Holler if you find anything."

Shannon went down the alley toward the rear. It was very dark, and he slipped the Colt out of its holster as he cautiously approached the store's back door. Abruptly, a trash can that he had just passed tipped over with a loud crash. Shannon crouched and whirled, cocking the six-gun. A half-starved dog was scurrying away up the alley, holding something in its mouth that it had found in the trash can. Feeling very foolish, Shannon returned the can to its upright position and went on to inspect the door. It was securely locked, so he replaced the Colt in its holster and started back around the building to the main street.

When he reached the boardwalk, Steve Warren was no longer there.

"Steve?" Shannon called in a stage whisper. "Steve, where are you?"

A single shot echoed out of the Yellow Dog Saloon across the street. A terrible premonition gripped Shannon as he drew his six-gun again and went pounding across the dark street toward the saloon. He flattened himself against the front of the building and moved up to one of the saloon's plate glass windows, intending to look inside. Just as he reached the window, the glass exploded outward and the body of a man came flying through it, knocking Shannon to the sidewalk. Half-stunned, Shannon struggled to his feet and looked dazedly around him. Broken glass was everywhere, covering the walk and the figure that lay still upon it. Lamplight flooded out through the broken window, and Shannon saw even before he rolled the body over that it was Steve Warren. He had been shot once in the chest.

Seeing that Warren was still breathing, Shannon placed his arm under the wounded man's shoulders and raised him up. Warren opened his eyes and looked at him.

"Mother . . . told me . . . be dentist. . . ." he whispered. The pain-filled eyes went blank, and the labored breathing stopped.

From inside the saloon, laughter was floating out into the night. *They're laughing about it,* Shannon thought. *That scum just killed Steve Warren, and they're in there laughing about it.*

He rose and started for the swinging doors, but before he reached them the Yellow Dog's bartender came dashing out.

"Don't go in there, Marshal," he said. "They're waiting for you. It's a trap."

"Who's in there?" Shannon asked.

"About twenty Diamond M riders," the bartender said, staring at Warren's body. "Almost the whole outfit, I guess. That foul-mouthed foreman of theirs, Horrocks, is with 'em. So's Bo Clagg."

"Clagg's in there?"

"Yeah. The whole thing was his idea. They watched for you, waiting for you to make your rounds. They saw you coming down the walk across the street, and Clagg sent a man out to say there was a fight in the saloon and you were to come quick. But Warren came instead of you."

Shannon bowed his head. He and Warren had ignored Hollister's warning to stay together, and Steve Warren had paid for it with his life.

"Who shot Warren?" he asked.

"Clagg did. Warren walked in and started to say something to him, real friendly-like, and Clagg shot him. He didn't have a chance."

Just like my father, Shannon thought. *He forgot to expect the unexpected.*

"It was awful, Marshal," the bartender said. "After Clagg gunned him, Warren tried to make it to the door, but he went down before he could get to it. I started to go over and help him, but before I could do anything, those varmints picked him up and tossed him right through the window."

"Why are you telling me all this?" Shannon asked. "You work here. Aren't you afraid Rufe Tittle will fire you?"

"He don't have to fire me, Marshal," the bartender said, taking off his apron. "I just quit. I ain't got no love for you deputies, but I don't hold with murder."

Footsteps sounded behind Shannon on the boardwalk. He wheeled around, his six-gun cocked and ready. Hollister and Bonham came running up. Shannon told them what had occurred.

Hollister uttered a strangled oath and bent over Warren.

"It's no use," Shannon said. "He's gone."

Hollister's shoulders sagged, and he began to curse bitterly under his breath. The others watched helplessly, shocked by Warren's death.

"I'm going in there," Shannon said, again starting toward the swinging doors.

"Don't do it, Marshal," the bartender said. "I tell you there must be twenty of them, and they're waiting for you, just spoiling for a fight."

"We're spoiling for a fight too," Bonham said. "I'm with you, Clay."

"Hold it," Hollister rasped. "If we go rushing in there, we'll be doing exactly what they want us to do. Let's use our heads about this."

He went up to the broken window and cautiously looked in, then returned to where the deputies were standing.

"Come on," he said, "let's get out of the line of fire. We're sitting ducks out here."

They told the bartender to go to the marshal's office and summon Walt Tucker. Then they dragged Warren's body off the walk into the alley and retreated across the street into the shadows on the other side, all the while carefully watching the saloon's door and windows. They half-expected the Diamond M men to come charging out after them, but no one appeared. The revelry within the saloon continued unabated.

"Celebrating, I'll bet," Bonham said. His features were dark with anger.

"Yeah," Hollister said, "and waiting for us to walk into the trap too."

Walt Tucker came hurrying up, despite his game leg and Shannon explained to him what had happened. Shannon could see that the news hit Tucker hard. He had worked with Steve Warren for several years.

"Okay, Bob," Tucker said grimly when Shannon had finished. "So Steve's dead. What are we going to do about it?"

"Shannon," Hollister said, "untie those horses from the hitchrail in front of the saloon and run them off. Be as quiet as you can. With all that noise inside, they may not hear you."

"What then?" Bonham asked, checking the chambers of his six-gun.

"Walt," Hollister said to Tucker, "when Shannon

has turned the horses loose, you and I will cross the street and join him. Shannon and I will go into the Yellow Dog through the front door while you cover us through that broken window. If anybody makes a move, shoot them."

Tucker drew his revolver.

"A pleasure," he said.

"What about me?" Bonham asked.

"You go around to the back of the saloon," Hollister told him. "Try to open the rear door without anybody noticing you. Watch until you see Shannon and me coming in the front way. Then go in and cover us from the back part of the room. Better move to one side as soon as you're in so we won't plug each other when the shooting starts."

Bonham slipped away up the street a few yards, then crossed and disappeared down the alleyway toward the rear of the saloon.

"Okay, Shannon," Hollister said. "Get the horses. We'll cover you from here. If anybody comes out of the saloon or tries to take a shot at you from the door or windows, drop down behind that water trough while we discourage them."

Shannon waited until he was certain no one inside the Yellow Dog was watching the street, then started across, crouching low with six-gun in hand.

The stupid clods, he thought, *they're not even keeping a lookout. Probably too drunk. Or maybe they're satisfied just to wait until we come busting in.*

He reached the hitchrail and began untying the Diamond M horses. As he loosed each one, he shooed it away from the saloon. Puzzled by their sudden freedom, the animals hesitated, then moved slowly off down the street. Shannon held his breath until they were gone, fearing the men in the saloon would hear the sound of their departure.

The concern for stealth was wasted, however. As Shannon stepped up onto the boardwalk to wait for Hollister and Tucker, hoofbeats filled the street and a dozen horsemen came galloping up from the direction of the stockyards. Shannon saw that they were the from the Box Y. Their foreman, Lon McLean, was in the lead.

The Box Y men reined up noisily and leaped out of their saddles, drawing their rifles from their saddle scabbards as they dismounted. They spread out along the street, taking positions in doorways and behind posts, boxes, and barrels as they leveled their weapons at the Yellow Dog Saloon.

Shannon ran out to intercept McLean as he was directing the deployment of the Box Y men. He hustled the foreman up onto the boardwalk and out of the line of fire from the saloon.

"McLean," he said, "what the devil are you doing here?"

"We got a score to settle with the Diamond M, Shannon," McLean replied, levering a cartridge into the chamber of his rifle. "I warned you people to keep out of our way."

"We've got a score to settle too," Shannon said. "Those vultures in the saloon ambushed Steve Warren tonight and killed him. We're going in after them. Don't interfere."

"I'm sorry about Warren," McLean said, "but this is our show. Pull out."

"Too late for that," Shannon said. "Look."

The noise had stopped in the Yellow Dog Saloon. Human silhouettes could be seen gathering at the door and windows. Someone smashed out the glass of the saloon's second front window, and rifle barrels came poking through the frame.

"Get back," Shannon said, pulling McLean up against the wall. "They've finally figured out there's something going on out here. No wonder, with all the noise you people made coming up."

Marshal Hollister joined them against the wall.

"McLean," he said, "get your men away from here. There are a couple of dozen Diamond M people in that saloon, and they're ready and waiting for us. If you go in there now, you'll start a full-scale war and get your whole outfit killed."

"Don't worry, Marshal," McLean said, "I'm not that crazy. We've got reinforcements on the way."

Shannon opened his mouth to ask what reinforcements he was talking about, but just then a Diamond M man caught sight of one of the Box Y riders across the street and fired. The Box Y cowhand gasped and fell, clutching his leg. Immediately, all of the Box Y riflemen started shooting at the saloon. Splinters flew from the window frames and doorway of the Yellow Dog, and inside the saloon someone began screaming.

"Let's get out of here before your men kill us too," Hollister said, grabbing McLean by the arm and starting across the street through the hail of gunfire. Shannon waited, covering them and holding his breath until they had reached the other side in safety. He was about to follow them when a Diamond M man stuck his head out one of the broken windows and saw Shannon crouched against the wall. He swung his rifle around to shoot, but Shannon thumbed the hammer of his six-gun and the man dropped the rifle and fell backwards out of sight.

The other defenders of the Yellow Dog, now alerted that one of the enemy was on the walk just outside the saloon, began ducking quickly out to fire at Shannon and then just as quickly jumping back inside to avoid the shots from the Box Y rifles across the street.

Shannon retreated hastily around the corner of the saloon, just as Bonham came running up the alley.

"What's all the shooting?" he asked. "It sounds like Custer's Last Stand."

Shannon pulled him back against the wall of the saloon and outlined the situation.

"We can't do anything about it from here," Bonham said. "We'd better get across the street where we can see what we're shooting at."

"I have to go inside," Shannon said. "Bo Clagg's in there. He shot Steve Warren and tried to kill me. I want him."

"Wait a minute," Bonham said. "I think the Box Y men are getting ready to charge the front door."

Shannon saw that Bonham was correct. Lon McLean was gathering his forces and pointing at the door of the Yellow Dog. The Box Y men started to cross the street, but a hail of fire from the saloon cut down two of them as soon as they left the covered walk. Their attack thwarted, McLean and the remainder of the Box Y riders pulled the downed men to safety and then resumed shooting at the saloon from the protection of the opposite boardwalk.

"It's a standoff," said Bonham.

"Not for long," Shannon said. "The Diamond M people will either launch an attack out of the front of the saloon, or escape through the back door."

"If they try to go out through the back they won't get very far," Bonham said. "I blocked the door. They can't get it open."

The fire from the Yellow Dog began to increase in volume.

"They must have an arsenal in there," Shannon muttered. "They're burning ammunition like they have a ton of it to spare."

Bonham was peering around the corner.

"You were right, Clay," he said. "I think they're getting ready to come out after the Box Y."

"It'll be a slaughter," Shannon said. "We've got to do something. I'll go out front and try to talk the Diamond M into giving up. You cover me from here. Hollister's across the street. He'll get the Box Y to hold fire."

"Don't be an idiot," Bonham said. "Those polecats in the Yellow Dog will cut you down the minute they see you."

"It's worth a try," Shannon said. He holstered his six-gun and started to leave the shelter of the alley. Belatedly it dawned on him that what Bonham had said was true. It was suicide. Even assuming that the other Diamond M riflemen didn't shoot him on sight, if Clagg spotted him from the Yellow Dog's windows he'd finish what he'd started that morning when he tried to bushwhack Shannon.

But I can't stop now, Shannon told himself. *I said I was going out there, and I've got to do it. Besides, I don't want McLean and the rest of the Box Y to be shot down. They're badly outnumbered, and if the Diamond M gunmen decide to rush them, they'll all be killed.*

"Blast it, Shannon," Bonham said, clutching at Shannon's arm, "if you walk out there, you'll die."

Shannon shook him off and moved out onto the boardwalk.

But he did not die, for events overtook him. As he stepped onto the boardwalk he became conscious of a distant rumbling, as if a thunderstorm were approaching. The rumbling grew louder, and Shannon realized suddenly what it was.

From around the next corner, a solid wall of longhorn cattle came hurtling up the street. Behind them more Box Y riders appeared, firing their guns into the air to urge the frightened animals on.

A stampede, Shannon thought. *So that's what McLean meant when he said reinforcements were coming.*

The running cattle were now almost abreast of the Yellow Dog. The street was crammed from walk to walk with an ocean of swaying horns, and the bellowing of the steers joined with the gunfire in a raucous symphony of noise. As the herd approached the front of the saloon, several of McLean's men who had been crouching on the boardwalk ran out into the street and began firing their weapons into the air also. The startled cattle, finding themselves assaulted from both ahead and behind, did exactly what the Box Y had intended them to do. They turned aside from their headlong charge and began leaping up onto the board-walk, frantically trying to escape the gunfire that threatened them from both directions. Looking across the street from his vantage point in the alley, Shannon could see Hollister, Tucker, and the Box Y men scattering to evade the horns and hooves of the maddened animals that were now filling the covered walkway.

On the side of the street where Shannon was standing, the panic-stricken cattle were crashing violently into the front walls of the Yellow Dog Saloon. Several of the longhorns discovered the open doorway of the saloon and plowed through it into the saloon itself. Yelps of dismay could be heard from within as the Diamond M men found themselves in the middle of an indoor stampede.

The Box Y hands were now all out in the street, shooting into the air and trying to head the cattle toward the Yellow Dog side. As Shannon watched in amazement, several more of the animals fled through the door into the saloon, and others, by now hard-pressed against the outside wall, began leaping in through the large broken windows.

Shots could be heard from inside the saloon as the Diamond M riders tried to fend off the cattle that were running about the room, but there was no longer any gunfire from the Yellow Dog's door or windows.

Some of the steers broke through the line of Box Y riders and came loping down the alley where Shannon and Bonham were standing. The two lawmen threw themselves back against the wall to avoid being trampled. One of the animals barreled into Cash Bonham, knocking him down.

"Are you all right?" Shannon asked, bending over him.

Bonham was holding his right wrist and gritting his teeth in pain. One leg was twisted under him.

"Think my leg's busted," he said. "Wrist too." He tried to get up, then sank back to the ground, gasping for breath. "Sorry, Clay," he said disgustedly. "Looks like you're on your own."

One of Bonham's six-guns had fallen to the ground nearby, and Shannon retrieved it for him. Then he helped the injured deputy to a nearby doorway, out of the path of any further loose cattle.

"You'll be all right here," Shannon said. "I have to leave you now. I've got an appointment to keep."

Bonham nodded.

"Good luck," he said. "If you find Clagg, say hello to him for me before you blow his brains out."

Shannon ran back down the alley toward the rear of the saloon. All he could think about was Clagg trying to ambush him and then treacherously shooting Steve Warren down in cold blood. *I should have killed Clagg when I had the chance,* Shannon told himself. *I won't make that mistake again.*

As Bonham had said, the rear door of the saloon was blocked with boxes and barrels. Shannon wrestled them aside, then cautiously opened the door. Beyond was a small storeroom, and Shannon advanced warily through it to a second doorway that was covered by a dusty curtain. He pulled the curtain aside and found himself confronted with a scene of utter bedlam. The saloon was filled with gunsmoke. Terrified cattle were plunging about, smashing tables and chairs as equally terrified men scrambled to get out of the way. The noise was deafening, a combination of shouting men, gunshots, the bellowing of the steers, and the crash of splintering wood. Only half a dozen men were still on their feet. The rest lay scattered about the saloon, bleeding from gunshot wounds or crushed by the cattle.

As Shannon watched, first one man, then a second, dodged away from the hooking horns and ran toward the door of the storeroom. Shannon ducked back into the storeroom, flattened himself beside the doorframe, and brought the barrel of the Colt down sharply on the head of each man as he came through the curtain. Leaving the two unconscious figures lying on the floor, Shannon pushed through the curtained doorway into the main room of the saloon. As he looked about, he saw that the few remaining Diamond M hands were now fleeing up the rickety stairway to the gallery above the saloon's main floor. They dashed through the doors that lined the gallery and disappeared. *They'll probably try to climb out the second floor windows,* Shannon thought. *No need to worry about them. Hollister and Tucker or the Box Y people will get them. But where's Bo Clagg?*

As if in answer to his question, Clagg popped up from behind the bar where he had been hiding and ran blindly toward the doorway in which Shannon was standing. In his panic, Clagg did not recognize Shannon until he was almost upon him. When he saw who it was, Clagg skidded to a stop, wide-eyed with surprise. His hand went to his holster, but the holster was empty.

"Lose something, Clagg?" Shannon asked, raising the Colt.

Clagg goggled at the rotating cylinder of the revolver as Shannon thumbed back the hammer.

"No!" he squealed. "Don't kill me! Give me a chance!"

"Like you gave Steve Warren?" Shannon asked. "Or like you gave me when you tried to backshoot me from that alley this morning?"

A rampaging longhorn came snorting by, narrowly missing Clagg. He flinched but did not move from the spot where he was standing.

"Come on, Shannon!" he pleaded. "Let me out of here!"

"You can leave any time," Shannon said. "All you have to do is get by me."

Clagg looked around in desperation.

"You got to give me a chance!" he cried again. "You can't just gun me down!"

Shannon hesitated. He wanted to pull the trigger and end Clagg's life then and there, but something inside him wouldn't let him kill an unarmed man. One of the men he had struck as they ran through the door had dropped his revolver on the floor near the doorway, and Shannon bent over and picked it up.

"Left hand," Shannon said. "Put it in your holster nice and slow."

Clagg goggled at Shannon as he took the six-gun with his left hand and awkwardly slid it into his holster, then watched as if mesmerized as Shannon holstered his own weapon.

"You don't deserve a chance," Shannon said, "but because I'm not like you, I'm going to give you one." He sidestepped as another steer charged by. It bolted through the doorway to the rear and Shannon could hear it rushing about in the little storeroom.

"Whenever you're ready, Clagg," Shannon said, "just go for that six-gun."

"This isn't fair," Clagg sniveled. "I've seen you draw, Shannon. You're faster than me."

Shannon's smile was deadly.

"Go for the gun, Clagg," he said. "I'll wait for you to draw, but when you do, I'm going to kill you. And if you don't draw, I'm going to kill you anyway."

"No!" Clagg screamed. "No!"

He turned and fled up the stairway to the gallery on the second floor. Shannon decided to shoot him in the back, then thought better of it and sprinted up the stairs behind him.

Clagg ran down the length of the gallery, looking apprehensively back over his shoulder at Shannon. At the end of the gallery, Clagg stopped and began trying frantically to open the door there. The door was locked. Clagg yanked repeatedly on the unyielding knob, blaspheming foully.

Shannon had followed him down the gallery and was now standing only a few feet away.

"It's no use, Clagg," he said. "This is the end of the line for you."

Clagg screeched in fright and tried to draw the revolver Shannon had given him. In his haste he bungled the draw and the six-gun went bouncing away over the gallery rail. Clagg looked wildly at Shannon once more, then turned and plunged headlong over the wooden railing, shrieking as he fell. He landed in a heap on the floor below and lay there, moaning. Shannon raced back down the stairs. Clagg was now trying to get up, crying out in pain as he did so. He reached his feet just as Shannon appeared once more in front of him.

"Nice try, Clagg," Shannon said. "Now, where were we?"

"I'm hurt!" Clagg whimpered. "I think my ankle's broke."

"Don't worry," Shannon said. "In a few seconds you're not going to be feeling a thing." He picked up the fallen six-gun and replaced it in Clagg's holster. Then he stepped back and reholstered the Colt.

"Ready?" he asked. "Good. Draw or die."

"Don't do it!" Clagg howled. "Don't!"

Completely crazed with fright, Clagg began backing through the pandemonium of the saloon toward the front door. A longhorn knocked him down, but he scrambled up again and continued his retreat, all the while watching Shannon with terror-stricken eyes. Looking beyond Clagg toward the front door, Shannon saw that the boardwalk outside the doorway was still choked with struggling cattle.

"You can't get out that way, Clagg," Shannon said. "Now draw, or I'll kill you where you stand."

Clagg uttered a final wail of fear and bolted blindly toward the front door. Shannon leaped after him, the Colt now in his hand. Before he could fire, Clagg had flung himself out the through door into the sea of swinging horns. Immediately he was swallowed up in the maelstrom. Shannon heard him screaming as he went down beneath the flashing hooves.

Shannon lunged for the doorway and paused there, trying to find Clagg in the seething mass. The stampeding longhorns had already charged into two of the posts that held up the roof over the boardwalk, shattering them, and the roof was now sagging badly. As Shannon stared at the swaying wall of flesh, trying to locate Clagg, another steer crashed into a third post, snapping it like a straw. Deprived of the last of its support, an entire section of the roof came smashing down onto the backs of the unfortunate cattle, causing them to redouble their efforts to escape and mercifully hiding the ugly scene from Shannon's view.

Chapter Nineteen

"Yeah, it's Clagg all right," Tucker said. "Or at least what's left of him."

The cattle had gone, the gun battle was over, and Shannon and Tucker were sorting through the wreckage of the fallen boardwalk roof.

Shannon looked among the splintered boards at the spot where Tucker was standing.

"Are you sure?" he asked. "It's hard to tell."

"Yeah, it's him," Tucker said. "I recognize the shirt."

Marshal Hollister came up to them. He looked weary and his face was streaked with dirt and perspiration.

"We've got the Diamond M survivors under arrest," he said. "I've temporarily deputized McLean and some of the Box Y men, and they're hauling the prisoners down to the jail."

"You're taking a chance deputizing the Box Y,

aren't you, Bob?" Tucker asked. "They're almost as mean as the Diamond M men."

"Almost," Hollister said with a laugh, "but not quite. Anyway, the Box Y saved our hides tonight. If the four of us had gone into that saloon alone, chances are we'd never have come out. Don't worry. I've told McLean and his whole outfit to head back to Texas after they've turned the Diamond M bunch over to Zeke and Packy at the jail."

He wiped his face with his handkerchief.

"Did you find Clagg?" he asked.

"Yes," Shannon said, pointing. Hollister grimaced.

"Has anybody seen Horrocks?" he asked. "He wasn't among the ones we arrested."

"He's inside the saloon," Tucker replied. "He won't be bothering us again."

"What about Cash Bonham?" Shannon asked. "Is he all right?"

"Fractured leg and wrist," said Hollister. "Doc says he'll be fine in a few weeks. He's hurting some, but mostly he's just mad that he didn't get a chance to go into the saloon with you."

"I don't suppose Councilman Tittle's going to be very pleased about the condition of his saloon, is he?" Shannon mused, looking at the wreckage.

"You needn't concern yourself over that," Hollister said with satisfaction. "I've already had a word with the right people regarding what went on here, and I guarantee you that Tittle won't dare to open his mouth about it. In fact, there are enough people who are unhappy with him right now that I don't think we'll be hearing much from him anymore. Political influence works both ways, as old Rufus is about to find out."

The undertaker and his assistant were busily moving among the still forms that littered the boardwalk and street. The three lawmen watched impassively as the morticians went about their work. Shannon knew he should feel some sort of remorse for Clagg and the other Diamond M dead, but somehow he could not. *They came to kill,* Shannon thought, *and they paid the price. Good riddance.*

Now that the shooting was over, a large crowd of people had gathered to stare at the corpses, the bullet-pocked saloon, and the shattered ruins of the fallen boardwalk roof. Shannon, Hollister, and Tucker silently wended their way through them. It occurred to Shannon suddenly that he was very, very tired.

Chapter Twenty

When Shannon came down the stairs from his room the next morning, Marian Thomas was not at the hotel desk. He looked in the dining room and then in the hotel kitchen, but there was no sign of her. He went back into the lobby and found the girl's father in his office, putting some things in a valise.

"Where's Marian, Mr. Thomas?" he asked.

"She's upstairs packing," Thomas said. "We're leaving today."

"Leaving?" Shannon asked. "Why?"

"I'm taking her away," Thomas replied. "I don't want her to spend her life in a dingy little room in a hotel in a cattle town. Especially this particular cattle town."

"But what does Marian think about going?" Shannon asked, trying to absorb the news of Marian's imminent departure.

"It was her idea, son," Thomas said softly. "She doesn't want to stay here anymore."

Marian Thomas came down the stairs. She was wearing a straw hat and carrying a suitcase. She paused as she saw Shannon, then continued down the steps.

"What's this about you leaving?" Shannon asked.

"I have to," the girl replied, wiping her eyes with a small lace handkerchief. "Even if I could stand this town, I couldn't stay here any longer because I care for you too much."

Shannon found himself momentarily speechless.

"I guess this time I'm the one who doesn't understand," he said.

"It's really very simple, Clay," Marian Thomas continued in a broken voice. "I love you. I guess I have from the moment I first saw you. And I don't want to sit around this awful place day after day waiting for you to be gunned down out there in that dirty street by some drunken cowboy."

Shannon groped for something to say. He hadn't consciously thought about Marian in terms of love. In truth, he hardly knew her, yet suddenly he realized that he was going to miss her very much.

"But if you love me, surely that's the best reason in the world to *stay*," he said.

"No it isn't," Marian replied, picking up her suitcase. "It's the best reason in the world to *go*. Goodbye, Clay. I wish you the best of everything, always."

She gave him a tiny, tearful smile and followed her father out of the hotel.

Clay watched in consternation as she disappeared from view. His mind was a whirlpool of conflicting emotions.

Walt Tucker had come into the lobby and had heard the exchange between Shannon and the girl.

"That's too bad, Clay," Tucker said. "I'm sorry it didn't work out for you. But don't worry. There'll be others."

"I don't know about that," Shannon said wistfully. "She was special."

"They're *all* special," Tucker said gently. "Every single one of them. You'll see."

He took out his watch and checked the time.

"Come on, son," he said. "Another trail herd's due in today, and we've got work to do."

Shannon walked slowly out the door, still trying to make sense of it all. As he stepped into the street, the star on his chest shone brightly in the morning sun.

Epilogue

The memories of his youth faded away, and Clay Shannon found himself once more in the garden at Rancho Alvarez with his wife Charlotte sitting close beside him. The scent of the flowers was still strong, but the moon was setting now, and there was a slight chill in the air. Shannon realized with a guilty start that he had talked well past midnight and into the early hours of the morning.

"I'm sorry," he said, putting his arm protectively around Charlotte. "I didn't mean to ramble on like that. Please forgive me. Would you like to go inside now?"

Charlotte shook her head.

"Not yet," she said. "Let's stay here a little longer."

She moved still closer to him and rested her head on his shoulder.

"So that's how it all began," she said thoughtfully. "It explains many things, doesn't it?"

183

"Too many, probably," Shannon said glumly. He glanced down at her, wondering if in talking about his past he had given away too much of himself, revealed things about himself that had shocked or repelled her.

Sensing his apprehension, Charlotte lifted her face and kissed him.

"Don't worry, Clay," she said softly. "What you've told me only makes me love you more, because it helps me to understand you, to understand the man who came to New Mexico to help a stranger, and stayed to rebuild Rancho Alvarez and share my life with me."

Shannon stood up, struggling to hide his emotions in the darkness of the garden.

"We'd better go in," he said, taking her hand. "It's late."

"But you haven't finished yet," Charlotte said. "You've only told me about Dry Wells and Longhorn. There were many years after that, many adventures in many places, before we finally met."

Shannon nodded. There had indeed been many years after Longhorn, years of carrying the star, years filled with violence and loneliness and sometimes even despair, before Fate had finally set him on the road to the town of Whiskey Creek and his meeting with Charlotte Alvarez.

"Yes," he said, as they moved slowly together through the starlit garden. "Yes, there's more I should tell you about, I suppose, things you're entitled to know. But let's save that for another time, shall we?"

They walked hand in hand into the house, leaving the garden and its memories to the night.